Letter from the Author

First and foremost, I want to point out that God made all living creatures in the beginning. All the animals on land and those living in the seas. He made the creatures that crawl and the creatures that fly in the air. At the end of each day, He says that He saw it, and it was good. I know dragons have always been depicted as a creature of evil but I would like to think that God made them first for good. Like humans, we were made to walk in the garden with Him. We were made in His image and we were made for good things. Then the darkness of evil came in and manipulated us out of His Grace. There are accounts of many wild and crazy creatures throughout the Bible. Everything from coiled-up Leviathans in Job to the seven-headed serpents in Revelations. God has created some amazing life and even though we don't have dragons flying through the air today, I do believe that they once did live and breathe. But in this story, these creatures and their stories are fiction replicating so many likenesses of our human truths. If there is anything that God says in this book can also be found in God's Scripture. If you feel that you need help realizing God's Truth of His Word in your life, then go to our website, www.Mark413.com, and send us a private message. We would love to help you walk in His Truths for your life.

Parts of these dragons can be represented in each of us. The Light and the darkness can come out at any given time. In every situation, we can decide to do good in this world or we can decide to do bad. We can always choose who we want to be because God gives us free will to be who want to be. (Deuteronomy 30:19-20) To worship Him and be in the Light or to worship evil and be in the dark. But in God's Word, He tells us that we can be hot or we can be cold. We can be good or we can be bad, but to be both disgusts Him. He will say that He does not know us and He will spit us out of His mouth. (Revelation 3:15) Let me inspire you to Believe in God again.

Let me inspire you to be the Light. (Matthew 5:14-16)

I have seen so many people who are like these dragons. They have been torn down in their life and have been manipulated to do evil instead of good. But let us read these stories like a child. In awe of God and all His wonders. Remember what got you excited about who God is. It is His love and how He leads us to our own truths through His Works. Let us remember our first love, like a child, let us applaud His Goodness and boo the bad guys as they are defeated in the end. Let us remember that like these dragons we have a story to tell and a seed that still needs to be planted to help share the gospel. Let us set our hearts on fire to share God's goodness through our own tales and never forget who our lives were meant to glorify. " Saying with a loud voice, Worthy is the Lamb that was slain to receive power, and riches, and wisdom, and strength, and honor, and glory, and blessing." Revelations 5:12

Dedication

To My Light Bearer, Paul.

You are more than my rock.

You are the example of God's Light that can be reflected.

You continue to teach me every day
How to Let My Light Shine Bright.

I Love You.

<3

Read Like a Child...

But Jesus said, "Let the little children come to Me, and do not forbid
them;
for of such is the kingdom of Heaven."
Matthew 19:14

Then war broke out in heaven. Michael and his angels fought against
the dragon, and the dragon and his angels fought back. But he was not
strong enough, and they lost their place in heaven. The great dragon
was hurled down—that ancient serpent called the devil, or satan, who
leads the whole world astray. He was hurled to the earth, and his
angels with him.
Revelation 12:7-9

So God created the great creatures of the sea
and every living thing with which the water
teems and that moves about in it,
according to their kinds,
and every winged bird according to its kind.
And God saw that it was good.
Genesis 1:21
* * *

Chapter 1: The Fallen Ones

Chapter Two: Then there was Light

Chapter Three: Alexander

Chapter Four: Ziggy

Chapter Five: Angelina

Chapter Six: Evil Crouching

Chapter Seven: Heaven Proclaims

Chapter Eight: No Savior

Chapter Nine: A Mind Manipulated

Chapter Ten: Truth in the Light

Chapter Eleven: Redemption's Hill

Chapter Twelve: The Battle

***

Chapter Thirteen: Judgment Seat

Chapter One: The Fallen Ones

1

Our story is often coiled with anger, fire, and blood. Whatever it is that you think you may know of us, you don't know our whole truth. You don't know the history of the darkness that lurked in the night to keep us from our true path. You may have heard of the tales of some of my ancestors. You may have heard some of their stories. Stories of how they represented the darkness and brought forth destruction and chaos as they killed many. But you did not know them before the darkness touched their lives. They have always been the ones flying through the clouds; hurting villages and pillaging golden treasures. Described by others as large scaly demon lizards who fly through the air in a furious rage to kill anyone that crosses their path. With impenetrable armor for skin and wings so large they could block out the sun. Their teeth are like jagged mountains and their claws are just as fierce. But that has not always been our purpose. To be killers; winged creatures of the night. Hateful selfish, gold-hoarding serpents bellowing hot gases and fire on all our enemies. That was not who God created dragons to be.

In Genesis, when God created the first Heaven. Then He created the Earth. He was hovering in between the lofts of the Heavens and He spoke. "Let there be Light" and there was Light. In that first burst of Light, we were born. We were created to serve God. We were created to protect Heaven. We were created to protect God's Beloved when they were laid to their final resting place and were able to enter through the gates of Heaven to be with God. When the first twelve dragons appeared in the beginning of time their sole purpose was to help God keep the darkness out of Heaven and to protect God's faithful creation. It is said that we were magnificent. There is no one like us on Earth. Our bodies are made of lean muscle, like etched stones. Our scales flowed in a gold-covered shield that covered our whole body. It was as hard as titanium and reflected God's Light with such radiance that it was hard to look at us if we flew in the sunlight. We could breathe out pure natural gas and with a click of our jaw, it would ignite into a pure blue flame that would turn anything into a pile of ash upon contact. Our wings could shield us from any enemy or any weapon and could cover the full length of our body from head to tail. We are magnificent creatures. We are Light Bearers. We are dragons.

In scripture, God speaks of Heaven which is built with streets of gold, stones made of rubies, and emeralds. That there are lakes full of all the tears God has collected from those He loves. He tells us that He's building us a mansion with many rooms in Heaven. That we will no longer want for anything. There will be a feast on a table just waiting for us. We will no longer have hurt, anger, pain, jealousy, rage, fear, torture, anxiety, sickness, or disease. There will be a throne room with four living creatures worshiping the Lord. There will be a multitude of angels and people standing before the Lord, worshiping Him. "Holy, Holy is the Lord!" The Heavens are our reward for being faithful to Him here on Earth. All the sacrifices we had made. The riches we gave away to help others. We would get it all paid to us when we got to Heaven to be with Him. To see His Face.

God has been with each of us since the beginning of time. The Holy Spirit is constantly calling us to the Lord. Calling us to open our eyes and to see the Light. As a dragon, we have felt His Presence since the beginning. Speaking to us and guiding us to do His Will. However, with each generation that lives and passes away, we have slowly turned our gaze away from Him. His Presence used to rule our hearts and guide our paths but is now fading into nothing. But just because few believe in Him doesn't mean He is not there. His power or strength does not decrease because we don't believe in Him. He was, is, and will always be. For now, He fills the Earth with His Presence, longing to be with us like He once was. The next generation needs to hear about God. They need to get to know Him again. They need to know Him and want Him more than they have ever wanted anything before. But how could we make a spoiled generation see that there is a greater purpose for their life aside from the path of torment and struggle they have created for themselves? My generation of dragons only knows how to kill, blow rages of fire, and destroy everything the humans have built. How do we tell thousands of dragons that their purpose in life is not to be like their parents and that their reason for living is protecting the very humans that they have only lived to kill? Lord, how did we become to be this unholy creature who only seeks more death and destruction?

He created us to protect His Beloved people when they reach their final destination in the mansion in Heaven. We were stationed all around the perimeters of Heaven to protect and watch over those who had finally made it home. The cliff perimeters were a large jagged stone edge that kept out the darkness. We are born on Earth so that we can get to know people. So we could learn who they were and have a healthy relationship with them. To guide them to God and to help them here on Earth. If a dragon followed the paths that God had laid out for them and mastered their spiritual gifts, then they were chosen by God to serve on the League of Protectors in Heaven with God. The angels lived there and choirs of millions were always singing His praises. God sat on His Throne and He has governed over all since the beginning of time. Once you came through the gates, you were never hungry, thirsty, or sleepy. There was no longer sadness, pain, or anger. There were waterfalls made of all the tears God had collected from the prayers of those still waiting to come home. You no longer had to worry about anything. You just had to rest and praise His name. In my dreams, I could see all the dragon ancestors on their stations, wings spread for full view. Reflecting God's Light to pour down onto the Earth. I can see the warmth they had for the people in their eyes. That kind of love could only be built on having a relationship with them. Serving with them. Protecting them. Their noble, statuesque faces lifted ever so slightly upwards facing towards God's throne. Heavenly proud creatures.

Unfortunately, when the Light was created the darkness was made known as the face of the darkness in the deep. Legends tell us that it was into that darkness deep inside the Earth that God sent The Fallen Ones when they were banished from the Heavens for trying to throw God off His throne. The darkness was a place absent of any light. Its walls were formed from the lava in the center of the Earth. Hard, rough crevices of fire and rock for miles as far as the eyes could see. Rivers of fire, rock, and ash streamed through the crevices; void of any life. One of our first ancestors was Drake. He was the first dragon ever to rise against God. Drake was a name and in the old language, it meant dragon. Drake thought he was better than the humans that he was created to protect. His vanity and pride clouded his mind. He rallied against God and got other dragons and angels to rise against God too. God banished Drake and The Fallen Ones to the darkness; never allowed to enter into Heaven again. They were cast down out of Heaven and they fell from the skies like a bolt of lightning. They were locked in the darkness in the fire and stone for thousands of years. God stripped away their armor and took away their gifts and magnificence. Their scales turned to a black, coal-like texture. No longer shiny and perfect. Their flame diminished to an orange fire because they no longer had access to living water. It would still cause damage but not like it used to. It no longer burns as hot. Their wings would take flight but only for shorter distances. Their eyes could no longer see the great distances that they once could. They could no longer hear each other through their thoughts. They could only hear through their ears. They could no longer talk to God or the other dragon protectors. Their hearing was limited to their close surroundings. In their case, lava and stone were all there was to hear moving. The spirits were immortal, so they would never die. The only way they could be killed was by another immortal being. However, God banished them to live in the darkness, causing even greater bitterness and anger in their hearts.

The stories tell us that it took him years, but Drake was able to dig himself out of the caves of darkness to get to the sunlight on the Earth's surface. He and the other three banished dragons could now roam the Earth with humans once again. However, once he realized that he was on Earth and could not get back into Heaven he became furious. His anger and hatred showed in everything that he did. He vowed to become greater and more powerful than God ever was. So he set out to gather all the human's gold, to cover his scales again. Hoping to achieve the glory that he once held. But no matter how much gold he plundered all he could, and all he could ever achieve was a mountain filled with gold and riches for him to sleep in. He could never eat enough cattle to get as strong as he once was. He could never drink enough water to quench his thirst. So in his anger, he roamed the Earth seeking to devour and destroy all living creatures and life. All he could think about was how mad he was at God for taking everything away from him. The more he would think about it the madder he would get. Eventually, he was consumed with so much jealousy and rage that it drove him to go on an unspeakable killing spree. Not killing just livestock and humans anymore but people say he killed the dragons he was banished with as well. No one knows for sure because their bodies were never seen. They were just gone from existence.

The times were beginning to change. People were moving faster than they used to. Daily life and the small details of their every day were getting less important to them each day. They want to spend less time working in the field and more time playing. They want to get paid more for things they don't make. They want more than they need. The methods to get them from place to place grew by extraordinary measures with every passing year. When the age settled to a place where God and the need for Him started to fade from their lives, Drake just disappeared in the night and hasn't been seen in close to a decade. His last attack was on a village in London and he wasn't successful at acquiring the gold from the building where it was protected. Some say that he died of old age. Others say that he died of a broken heart being cast out of Heaven away from God. But in the dead of night, you feel the darkness a little extra when the moon is small. The trees sway and crackle like his wings just brushed through them. All the creatures hide and go silent. As if they know something we don't. They can see things in the dark that we can't. Every creature's breath is shallow, like a featherweight rock skipping across the top of the water. Afraid to breathe deeper because then the darkness that was closing in would hear where you are. It's nights like tonight you know it is best if you just stay inside; stay where it is safe and where you can see everything. The shadows don't tend to play tricks on your mind inside. All you can do is breathe as shallow as possible and pray for the sun to rise again.

~ * ~

Drake had two league brothers and one sister who were cast out of the

Heavens with him. Alexander, Ziggy, and Angelina. It was harder for the other three to be cast away from God and when Drake went on his rampage after getting back to the surface, they could no longer stand to be near him. They immediately felt in their hearts that what they had done was wrong and they missed being in God's Presence. They quickly sought redemption from God; begging Him for forgiveness. God turned His face from them. Forbidding any of the other dragons to speak or help them. Because they can not fellowship with the darkness that had overcome them. Drake began killing and burning village to village. People's legends tell us that they saw the three fall out of sight in the skies, but no one knew exactly where they went. No one ever found their bodies. People say that they were killed by Drake because he was after all the gold for himself. But in my heart, I know they are still alive. I can feel their immortal spirits in mine. I think that they are waiting to find out what the cost of their redemption would be. Waiting to see if God will ever let them back into Heaven to be with Him again.

There are tales in China of great old dragons living harmoniously with humans. Helping, healing, and aiding people in any way they can. But it has been many years since they have been seen. Like most magical creatures they have vanished without a trace. Almost as if their lives faded away with their usefulness. Once people no longer needed them, they were no longer called upon and it is said they fell into a great sleep in the mountains. The Holy Spirit that was here on Earth helping people live righteously no longer glows with His same radiance. Technology and science appear to have enabled people the powers to no longer need God. It had appeared that the new technology of the world had made their use for all things spiritual or magical and rendered them useless. Their paths were now guided by their wants and desires instead of what was good for their life. Instead of doing all they could to get themselves to Heaven, they now longed to get a coffee or an elaborate destination for a vacation. Whatever made them happy now was all they asked for out of their life. There was no Heaven or Hell. There was no God or devil. There was no afterlife that they needed to worry themselves with.

A dragon to them was just another large animal they needed out of their way. The more people that believed that lie it turned the dragons against the people. Because with every dragon life that was disposed of, there was a dragon who was left hurt and alone. Enraged that their loved ones were taken from them. The magic that the dragons carried would die once they no longer lived here on Earth. When their bodies die here their spirit then goes to Heaven if they fought for good and for God. If they fought with Drake and for evil then they were to go to Hell and into darkness. Every spirit lives for an eternity. It is your choice as to where you will go when you die. You can choose to live in the Light with peace and tranquility. Or you can choose to live your life in fire and stone without God or the Holy Spirit to help you. It's your choice.

So the dragons who live today have lost everything that they once knew they were. They have lost their purpose, their joy of serving God, and the peace of knowing they were doing good for the Lord. Every generation of dragons that live is only living the lie that Drake and the darkness want them to believe is their truth. That their only reason for living is for killing, stealing, and hurting others. Hurting other dragons and humans alike. Because if he can get them to believe the lie then they will never become the dragons they were created to be. Holy, Righteous, and Pure. If he can get them so twisted in doing all the wrong things then he can keep them from being with God. Making his vengeance real and complete. Drake may not be able to be God's number one protector but if he couldn't, no one could ever replace him. If he could keep the humans from going to Heaven too well then that would just be icing on his cake.

The darkness has crept into their lives and enslaved them without them even knowing they were being held captive. Evil has made their jail cell so luxurious they no longer feel like they need to leave. In their cell, they believe their choices don't have meaning in the spirit. They think that the bad choices are only someone else's black-label of opinion. That their beliefs are outdated and not up to date with the age and that they can be whoever they want. Love whomever they want. Hurt whomever they want. Steal whatever they want. The powerful ones did what they wanted to, with no accountability. The poor justified their needs and their will to steal to get what they wanted. To them; there was no heaven or hell. There was no reason to believe in God. He was just some old deity their ancestors created to maintain peace. To help keep people in line. They could justify their reasoning with science and technology. Whatever they couldn't explain with those means they wrote off as coincidence. Dragons have lost who they are in God. They have forgotten how magnificent they could truly be. They forgot how wonderful it was to feel God's warmth radiate from the Heavens down on their skin. They have lost what it felt like to have God's help with every hard situation there was. After a while, all they felt was the struggle and now they were alone to figure it out for themselves. They stopped believing in the very One who could save them from all their frustration and torment. From their anger and their strife. From their despair and anxiety.

God longed to help them once more. He wanted to give them the peace they longed for and help them through their pain. But because He gave them free will, He gave them the ability to forget who He was and that saddened Him. God never wanted them to be away from His side. He often wished He could be with them in the cool of the day; talking and reminiscing of the days past. He wished they could have great adventures together again. He missed teaching them His Deep Knowledge of the universe that He had created. He missed their longing for knowledge and wisdom. He wished that He could teach them once more about who He had made them to be. That He could help them become who they were meant to be. It was going to be such a glorious day when they realized that they were created for more than the misery they were fighting through. When He created them, He envisioned these magnificent creatures reflecting all of His glory to the Heavens and down into Earth. That they would reflect His Love for all the creatures. They were created to glorify the Lord and to guide others to God. Ultimately to end their journey with Him in Heaven. That despite whatever darkness they would come across they could overcome the darkness with His power and love. God never thought that the darkness would ever have been allowed to grow into what it had become. However, it did have help getting there.

~ * ~

Each of the fallen dragons, except Drake, was born on Earth and had lived with people until God chose them to serve on the League of Protectors. The League was a specialized group of dragons to whom God had given spiritual gifts to govern Heaven as He wanted. It was such a blessing to be called to have a relationship with God. But to be chosen by God to serve in Heaven was an honor held in the highest regard. There were only twelve positions of honor that could be held in the League of Protectors. A dragon could only be chosen if they have overcome their mountains of struggles or fears, have kept their life in righteousness regardless of the evil they faced, and have mastered their spiritual gifts to glorify God. Then, and only then, could you be chosen. Each dragon carried one, often two of the spiritual gifts placed on their life by God. Each gift was different but their only main purpose was to glorify God in every life. Although, all twelve dragons have one or two of the gifts, sometimes the same gift can be in more than one dragon because of their experiences of their life.

Each gift was special, just like the life of the dragon that it was given to. With every soul that God breathed life into He has given a specific purpose and a plan for them to live. God is omnipresent and can see our lives in full. He knows everything there is to know about each dragon and the evils that he or she will be faced with in their lifetime. He is always with them and He always knows what they need to do before they need to do it. He has made a way when it appears that there is no way. He has laid the provisions and He has sent help to each dragon before they can even call out His name. It is their choice to call upon Him for His help.

All gifts are given to glorify God through those gifts. There is the gift of administration. Those gifted with this gift are skilled organizers and excellent task executors. There are some gifted with the gift of leadership and they are wonderful at pointing others to the Lord. There is the gift of discernment and this gift helps those who have the gift to know where their intentions are coming from. Some intentions can be good, bad, or of one's flesh. Those who carry the gift of discernment can tell us which master it serves. Some carry the gift of evangelism and the one who carries this gift excels at reaching out to those who are not saved and bringing them to become a believer. They are amazing communicators of the gospel and preaching about God. The gift of exhortation is often an encourager to others around them. They often are skilled at reminding others about the work that God is doing in their life. The spiritual gift of faith is someone who has been chosen to be given an extra portion of faith and trust in the Lord. They have an assured confidence that is in God to walk boldly with Him through their life. The gift of giving and have been abundantly blessed in God's favor and provision. So they tend to be the ones to give more of their time, money, and resources. In scripture, it tells us of nineteen spiritual gifts God gave us. Some of us have been endowed with all the gifts but often there are only a few gifts that are in us that are operating stronger than others.

As a dragon, our experiences in our life have molded our paths differently but we all are pointed to God for our salvation and love. We have been given the opportunity to give in to the temptations of evil and fall short of God's Glory revealed in us through free will. But we also have the chance to let God save us from that temptation to be evil and to do the good that He has called us to become. To be chosen for the League of Protectors every dragon has to overcome this darkness and become the Light to others. Drake was one of the original protectors that were created at the beginning of time. All he has ever known was God, as his father. He never had to live with people or learn how they do things on Earth. He never had the joy of helping them succeed. Or planting the fields or getting them ready to harvest in the fall. He has only ever cared for people after they had died and come home to Heaven. There was so much to learn about yourself through helping others through their trials and tribulations. When you are caring for someone else you can see your paths as they are laid out. The good path and the bad path that one could take. If you spend too much time alone, you tend to think only for yourself. What you need and what you want from others. As for Drake, who knows why he rebelled against God? Was it his pride that got the best of him? Or was it the jealousy that he could never be God?

It's hard to tell where the darkness crept into Drake's mind. But once it was allowed to take hold and simmer there as it began to warp every thought that he had. Those who were close to Drake could see something was bothering him. He started to become quiet and withdrawn from others. He stopped joining social events and turning down invitations from friends and students. The darkness wants to make you feel alone and unwanted. If it can get you all to itself then it can have its way with your mind. That's why God always tells us two are good but three is a cord that can never be broken. Friends can tell when there is something wrong. They can tell when you're not thinking about things the right way. We often wonder where Drake's friends were when he was pulling away. Why didn't any of them speak to him and ask him how he was doing? Regardless, the darkness will do everything in its power to keep your mind unaware of what it's doing. To keep you distracted from your cause will only further his. If it can keep you concentrated on feelings of despair and depression then it can keep you from helping others and being good. If it can keep you off your path of righteousness, then you will never have the chance to be chosen to be a part of God's Chosen League of Protectors.

Drake was never created to be the leader of The Fallen Ones. He was created to be a leader of the Light. God never created him to be in despair and loneliness. He was created for leadership and teaching other dragons to be better Light Bearers. God never wanted this life for Drake. God had great plans for Drake. Drake was living a life in Heaven that others were praying they could have. He was respected, and honored, and was a part of helping teach others how to be great as well. He had a wonderful life. He was loved. What temptation could have led him away from his life? This was not who Drake was supposed to be. Dragons were never meant to be who they had become. The time for worship was over and people and dragons were on a path of destruction that was soon going to kill all spirit life as we knew it. If someone didn't intervene. But who would stand against the darkness?

Chapter Two: Then there was Light

2

There was always a still small whisper in the air guiding us and keeping us safe. We could feel it there in the warmth of the Light during the day and a kiss of its presence in the warmth at night as we coiled up to go to sleep. We could hear God speak in the cool of the breeze. We could feel Him in the lift under our wings as the warm air helped us ascend into the clouds. Every dragon knew He was with them. Well, we knew something was with us. We may not have known it was Him directly yet but we knew something was calling us to the Light. Eventually, every dragon would have a relationship with Him. It was during this time together with Him in our secret place that each of us found our true purpose in this life. But each of our stories is different. He would reveal Himself to us in different ways and at different times in our lives. For some, He would come in a mighty force strengthening and empowering a life. For others, it was in the quiet. In the stillness of the moment, you could almost feel time slow down just enough to know He was there speaking to you. Helping you decide what to do next. You would never see anyone there speaking but you knew volumes more than you did a moment ago. Just like that, your quandaries were gone. You knew where you were supposed to go or what you were called to do.

The Holy Spirit is here in God's place till you and He can be rejoined in Heaven to help you through any trouble. He won't do it for you and He can't get involved on your behalf but He is there to provide you with comfort when you're scared. Strength for when you're weak. Guidance when you are unsure what you should do. Dragons have had him by our side ever since the veil was torn. You see there used to be a barrier between the heavenly realm and the Earthly realm. God's Holiness was not able to be around those who weren't clean; both physically and spiritually. So there were steps only a select few people would have to go through to make themselves clean so that they could go and humble themselves before the Lord to be in His Presence. It was the only way He would come down and speak with us after Adam and Eve sinned in the Garden of Eden. The veil was torn when God's Son, Jesus Christ died for our sins on the cross. When He did that, anyone can call on God the Father and talk with Him through His Holy Spirit.

Jesus was God who was born into a human body. He was pure and Holy. His life was lived without any sin and He was crucified for us all. He died on the cross and then rose from the dead to sit with God the Father in Heaven once again. But when He left us here, He told us He was leaving the Holy Spirit to be our guide to righteousness in His place. Without His guidance, we would not know our path to get to Heaven.

Jesus' death happened many years ago. So many that most have forgotten the ways our ancestors lived. Dragons and humans alike have lost the relationship with God that we once had. We have lost the purpose for our life. We have lost the need for our purpose. The humans think their life is to get up, work, make money, party, and then get old and die. Dragons aren't that much different. Get up find gold, kill, and set fire to villages and delight in the hurt that we have done for the day. Dragons have forgotten why God created them. When Drake and The Fallen Ones became jealous and prideful they walked away from their purpose. They no longer wanted to be who God wanted them to be. They wanted to be who they thought they should be. But what they didn't realize was that you couldn't obtain respect, righteousness, and holiness any other way without the help of God and his ways. It just wasn't possible. So when Drake and the Fallen Ones were cast out of Heaven they did whatever they wanted to do. But they soon realized honor, glory, and power could only come from God, the Father.

When Heaven was created when God said, "Let there be Light!" there were no dragons yet assigned to protect the Heavens from darkness. They were in Heaven but they did not know their purpose.

God assigned each of them to a portion of Heaven that was theirs to protect. He gave them gifts in their spirit man that could help them know what God would want them to do. They could discern which way to go to stay on the righteous path. When God sat down on His Throne. His Light illuminated the realm, pushed back the darkness, and kept it away. Wherever God was, darkness could not be. He cannot fellowship with darkness. Darkness tries with every fiber of its being to overcome the Light but it will never be powerful enough to do so. God's Light was enough to keep darkness away from us. As long as we stayed in His Light we would be okay. But all of the dragon's jobs were to reflect God's goodness everywhere they went to everyone they met.

With every dragon that was chosen to serve on the League of Protectors, they reflected God's Light across the Heavens and onto the Earth. Every new soul that came to believe in the Lord and His power in their life, then also became a carrier of God's Light shining bright for others to see. Every human and every dragon alike bears His Light. We carry His Light and bring His Glory to others around us each day. As a carrier, we are chosen to use God's gifts to bring others to the Light as well. The twelve dragons surrounding the Heavenly realm were all strong in God's gifts.

In Heaven, Drake was a gifted teacher. He excelled at communicating and he knew all things about God. He would dive into the scriptures and teach others how to have a more intimate relationship with God. He was the first dragon assigned and gifted, so he has been with God the longest. So he was the perfect dragon to teach us about God and what God was thinking. He was an amazing teacher. He was always mysterious enough to draw his students out of their nervous shells. He captivated his students to want to get to know God and inspired them to go after more of Him in everything they did. All to God be the Glory. Drake used his gifts to glorify the Father.

Drake also carried the Gift of Knowledge which allowed him to use the knowledge the Holy Spirit imparted to him to speak into other's lives. Which made him an even better teacher of all the things that were about God, our Heavenly Father. He could speak to the things that were not about God as well. So if you were straying away from Godly wisdom and off the path that God had set for you, then he could speak to your heart about the matter. Using his God-given spiritual gifts to bring others closer to God. In doing so, he gained power and honor from all those he taught. But when he was banished from Heaven he lost everything.

Over time, Drake became jealous and angry that the humans were more important to God than he was. Drake remembered being God's favorite dragon. His job was to lead the League of Protectors and the Angels in all their responsibilities. Dragons and humans honored him and respected him. His armor was the shiniest in all the Heavens. He was the example of who a dragon needed to become. To reflect God's glory, honor, and power in all the heavens and the Earth. All in Heaven honored him. All dragons on Earth wanted to be him. He was the shiny example of the dragon's purpose and life.

So when the darkness turned his honor into self pride and jealousy it was a shock to everyone. Drake used to give classes to the new trainees about how to watch out for the seed of darkness that could sneak up on you when you least expected it. Evil was manipulative. It comes into your mind and distorts your thoughts and ideas, so they are no longer pure and holy. It turns your motives to do something for good into something it shouldn't be. For example, you're excited about your friend who was just awarded a medal at the dragon ceremony for bravery. With a touch of darkness, your happiness for your friend is turned into jealousy and fear that you won't ever get an award. If you allow it to take root in your mind and heart it can cause you to do hurtful things toward your friend. That is why God teaches us to watch for the little foxes that can enter our vineyard. We think that a little fox isn't going to steal but a little amount of grapes. But before you know it, your whole vineyard has been picked dry and you have no grapes left to make any wine. If you allow darkness in to take a little from you he will turn it around and take it all. You will no longer be joyful about your friendship. Evil has come in and robbed you of all your joy. Stolen your friendship and killed your excitement for them. Just a little bit of darkness has ruined your whole day.

Drake allowed the darkness to take everything he had away from him. His pride and jealousy of God's Glory took his honor, glory, and power away from him. His pride turned into this ugly beast called arrogance and that took away Drake's job and respect. His jealousy turned into fear. Fear then begins to cause you to do whatever you can to hold onto the life you had built for yourself. But rarely does it ever work. Once he allowed jealousy to take hold of him he then lost any honor that was left in his heart. When that happens the downhill spiral has begun. Without honor, you lose all moral values of what is good. You then begin to justify everything you do from here on out. You reason that you don't need God. That He never did anything for you anyway. He was just a myth that your ancestors created to keep dragons in line with the rules. We can't see God, so therefore He doesn't exist. His love, honor, power, and relationship are now nothing more than a dream. A dream and a purpose are all gone in one bad decision.

So now Drake's sole point in his life is to cause as much death on the human race as he can. When he dug himself out of the pit of darkness and Drake realized he was on Earth with the humans he immediately was enraged. He snorted a cloud of gray smoke and took to the skies setting fire to anything he could. Trees, plants, houses, animals…It didn't matter. Within seconds everything he could see was a blaze of anger raging furiously. In Drake's mind, he may not be able to keep the humans from getting home to Heaven but he sure could make their lives harder here on Earth. When human life is finished here in the physical realm their bodies pass away but their spirit still lives. It is their spirit man that comes home to Heaven to be with God for eternity. Their home in Heaven is their reward for staying on God's path and living a life worthy of God's honor and love. Drake could go on a giant killing spree but that wouldn't stop them from joining God in Heaven.

That is when Drake plotted a plan to disrupt God's path for their life. If Drake couldn't kill them to keep them from God then he would manipulate them to take themselves off the path of righteousness. He planned to gather all the gold on Earth for himself. If there is no gold on Earth for the other dragons and humans then everyone will want it more. It will consume their lives. If everyone thinks there isn't any gold for them, then they will become frantic to get some for themselves. They'll work harder and longer to find some. They'll ignore their need to go to their secret place to spend time with God because they'll need their whole day to find more gold.

Drake's plan to keep the other dragons from God worked better than he anticipated. Dragons began seeking gold as if their life depended on it. The selfishness Drake activated throughout the Earth began a new reign of evil set forth on the world. Dragons hurting and killing dragons for their stash of gold. They became single-minded and after only one thing in their life ever again. The darkness took over them. Through the many generations of dragons who have come after have been only known as the lizards of the sky that they have become. Nothing more. Only after gold; a mineral that was created to reflect the Glory of God's Light through the skies. They have turned the mineral into material wealth only given to those who are powerful enough to get it. No matter the cost to the lives of those who seek it. Their hunger for gold consumed their every thought. Every thought. It changed the very fiber of who God made them to be. Eventually, the darkness was so deep and uncontrolled that it changed their family bloodline. It changed what they looked like and what they acted like. Their family's stories were altered to something they had never intended to be. They became a lost, bloodthirsty, gold-hoarding monster that could no longer be distinguished from evil. Synonymous with the darkness before God spoke light into existence.

The darkness before God's goodness was revealed. Before He gave us life. The darkness has corrupted the very foundation of who we were created to be. Now future generations have lost the truth of their identities; chasing after a false reward on Earth. Instead of going after God's reward by joining Him in the League of Protectors.

We have forgotten how great God's rewards were. We have lost the vein of His glory and His goodness in our blood. We have been held hostage against our will. Held captive by evil and the impurities that bad seeds have planted in our souls. I can only imagine how great it would have felt to be selected for the League of Protectors. The honor that was bestowed because of your loyalty and obedience. I imagine what it was like for God to help you put on your armor for the first time. Or for your gifts to be recognized by the Heavenlies. Everything about you being rewarded. Everything that your father said about you wasn't true. That you weren't good enough, or big enough, or smart enough to stand beside him. He always said there was something wrong with me because I couldn't fly as high as him or spit flames as hot as his. Or kill as many people as him. How could God see him worthy enough to stand beside Him? How could God ever forgive dragons for who they had become?

Some stories have been passed down through the ages of dragons who had been called to God and His righteous path. Not every dragon who is born is called to speak with the Holy Spirit. There are only a few called to be with Him in Heaven. It was a privilege to be called His. A dragon called to be God's they radiated a Light everywhere they went. Darkness could not penetrate their soul. The Light was too strong for the darkness to overcome them. In the stories, darkness said that the Light they carried was so powerful it could disperse the plans of evil just by calling on His name. A barrier would surround those to whom He loved and evil could not touch them. No matter what sorcery they spoke or magic they conjured. It was useless against those God called to His Side. I often played like I was a bearer of that Light when I was younger. I would imagine dispelling darkness and walking through the rubble I left behind by my Light stream. Me and God would go on grand adventures together taking down our enemies. We would fight side by side. Hand in Hand against the darkness that thought itself a formidable opponent. Only to be sadly mistaken when they faced us in battle. They were no match against us.

For as long as I can remember I have thought that I was misunderstood and that there was something wrong with me because I didn't want to be my father. My father sought those things like it was a sport. Rage and anger were the only emotions he could find joy in. I never knew what happened to my mother. She's never been in my life. I don't know if she is dead or alive. Part of me wishes to know where she was and then the other part of me feels she doesn't deserve to know me now. My heart tends to think that I must be more like her because I am nothing like my father. But I will never know. I don't want to know. My father sees a hurt man in the woods and he automatically goes in for the kill. I see a man hurt in the woods and my first instinct is to get him to safety, then find out what is wrong to heal him. We are worlds apart and I feel alone.

That is why I go to the cave behind the waterfalls. It feels so peaceful there. I can just be myself; alone with my thoughts and feelings. Whatever they may be. If my father had anything to do or say about the matter, he would say I wasn't being productive enough. If I hadn't set at least a few villages on fire he would torment me with phrases like, "I swear there is just something wrong with you! When I was your age I used to love to burn forests to the ground. Does Drake's blood not flow through your veins?" I would just cringe when he would tell me stories when I was younger about all the damage he and his father would cause. I would bow my head and feel bad for the families that had to deal with so much. My heart would ache for them. I could barely breathe thinking about all the hurt and pain they had to have felt. Loved ones-gone. Homes-gone. Pets-gone. The devastation had to have been unbearable.

When I would go to the cave for peace away from him, I could rest and imagine a life that didn't involve so much killing and loss. I could see myself giving the kids a lift from the watering hole back to their house. I would imagine that I would help the farmer down the road till up the ground of his garden and move heavy logs or rocks out of the way. I could always envision my strength being used for good instead of evil and hurt. My fire could light a stick for the Momma to light her home in the evenings. I could protect them from harm. My flight could help them get messages or aid to those they love far away. I could never understand why we had to hurt people. For the most part, people were just afraid of us dragons, but they didn't need to be. Not of me at least. I was intrigued by them. I wanted to know more about their lives and their families. I wanted to know how I could help them live better. With every fiber of my being, I longed to be good to them. Every time I would make this suggestion to my father he would answer to the effect that it was not the way our dragon ancestors taught us how to be. They would know. They were older and smarter than I was. He would belittle my thoughts and treat me as if I was unable to measure up to his caliber of thinking.

He always had this way of making me feel bad for even thinking about such thoughts. I felt like an outcast to my father. I often wondered if was he even my father because we were so different. One day in the cave, I was talking to myself, and out of nowhere, someone answered. I was questioning why his way had to be the only way for me to live. Complaining to the walls that I should just run away; that I could take care of myself. That I didn't need him. I was a full-grown dragon and could make my own decisions on who I should be. The next thing I knew, I was seeing a different life than the one I was living. I was flying over the treetops and I was protecting this group of people and I was helping them get to this settlement. I was wearing this armor that appeared to be reflecting light for them to see where they were going. My skin was clean and warm. I was wearing a protective shield on my head that sat on my horn tops and was secured under my chin. The people were so thankful for my help. The little kids ran up and hugged my tail. They brought me baskets of food to show their appreciation. I realized that what I was seeing was who I wanted to become. I felt so unworthy but my heart ached for it to be true with everything in me. Only my eyes showed the truth as the tears ran down my cheek.

The innocence of my childhood would be soon unraveled by my father's harsh laughter. He would torment me with jokes and riddles about my battles against the darkness. When I was young and naive I would get angry and yell at him that God and I could take on the world. That we were stronger than anything evil could throw our way. My arguments would soon tarry as I would get older and my father's words would grow with me. Somewhere along the way, my father sought me as his enemy that he needed to tear down with his hurtful quibs. When I became a teenage dragon I felt it was better for me to get away from him as much as I could. That's why the cave became so important to me. It became my solitary refuge away from his abusive voice. He always told me he was just turning me into a dragon that could take on the world one day. That one day, if I listened to him and his teachings, would become this undeniable, mighty force that no one could come against. But I didn't want to be evil. I didn't want to hurt others. I didn't want to kill for gold and hoard it in a mountain to sleep with my riches and treasures that were bigger than anyone else's. Too bad God didn't create a gift for those who liked to run away from their enemies, because I could definitely say I had that one mastered by now. My catchphrase for my superpower of good would be spoken right before I used my gift. "Then God said Let there be Light." Once I said that a Light would shine forth and heal the sick, free those being held against their will, and would be forever changed to want to do good from now on.

What we don't know is that there is a great multitude of variables that go into one single decision that needs to be made. We only see a choice of two different paths that we can choose to walk on. However, there was so much that you did not see that brought you to this point in your life. It all begins with our family bloodline and the choices that our ancestors made in their lives. The good and the bad choices gave them consequences that affected every family member down the line. One single selfish moment and your life was forever changed and after they pass on from this life they can no longer do anything to fix it. The course is set in stone and everyone is left to clean up the mess.

You don't feel that is true? Then you never had a disobedient, angry father. Or a bloodthirsty, killing uncle who watched you from time to time. Everyone in your family has affected your life in one way or another. Some good effects and some bad ones but is the effect that they could have on our life avoidable? Can it be stopped? Can you get away from all the hurt, pain, and devastation that your family has bestowed upon you? Do I have to live out the bad choices my family has brought my life to become? Just because my father is mean to people does that mean that I have to be? If my mother was dark and evil to other dragons, does that mean I have to be too? What if there is a reason that I am drawn to the light and that I want to be good and not evil? What could that reason be? Could I be my version of who a dragon should be? Could I help humans instead of killing them? Was I strong enough to bear the weight that being the dragon I wanted to be was going to bring me?

These were the questions I was speaking out loud in the cave when the Light appeared and spoke to me. I was young. I was nine years old and even though I had a wild imagination and a creative spirit I was still surprised and a little scared when God first appeared to me. I jumped and turned around to see who had just spoken to me. Out of nowhere, this electric floating blue glowing ball said, "Yes, Alastair. You can break the curses of your family bloodline."

I thought I had finally lost my mind and was seeing and hearing things, but nope. It was there and He was talking to me. To me? How did He know me? He called me by my name. Was He an alien? Where did He come from? Before I knew it He answered my questions again. "Alastair, I am not an alien. I am He. I am God, the maker of Heaven and Earth. I know you and I created you." His voice was so soothing to me.

Oh my goodness! God was here and He was talking to me! Me, Alastair. A nobody, a worthless dragon that couldn't do anything right. Wait!? What?!? How did He hear my thoughts? "I can hear your thoughts because I am He. I created you." He keeps saying that. That He created me. I don't know why that feels like there is something that

He's leaving out. It feels like there is a "but" coming at the end of that sentence…and if He is God, the Almighty. Why has He let this hurt and pain terrorize the people? Why doesn't He help them and protect them from dragons like my father? Wait! Why didn't He protect me from my father? I had so many questions that I just wanted answered. I sat down on the cold cave dirt floor and remained quiet, listening. "Alastair, just breathe. Sit with me for a while and let me tell you about the beginning of time."

I sat there and patiently listened as God began to tell me the intricate details of why He created Earth, the Heavens, and people. As intriguing as everything He was telling me was, I was so warm and comfortable with Him there with me. He was telling me His great plans that He once had for the League of Protectors and the humans in Heaven to live together in peace. Twelve dragons would be chosen to serve in this great army. We would be held in the highest honor. We would be given a new skin that would reflect God's Light everywhere. We would wear helmets that would be made of the strongest armor to protect us. Our scales would be individually plated of the same indestructible armor that no darkness could ever pierce. We would be stationed all around Heaven's perimeter to guard against evil coming anywhere close to God or His Beloved.

He was getting so excited talking about His plans for us all. I started to get excited with Him. He kept talking about humans with such love and grace. He would talk about some of the first days after He created them. How they would walk together for hours talking about the plans they had for the Garden. He talked about this one human, Adam, with such a warm heart. However, He also told me about how the darkness snuck in and stole the humans away from Him to hurt Him. He said that was a very sad day for Him because He had to curse him and his wife for disobeying Him. He said the relationship with humans has never been the same since then.

I felt bad for God having such a strained relationship with them. I wished there was something I could do to help. I asked God if there was something I could do to help and all He said was that I could help by staying on my righteous path for my future. I felt like there had to be more that I could do but He assured me that I was doing all He could ask of me. My thoughts were there with God but my heart couldn't let their relationship troubles go. When God was telling me the purpose of the lives of the League of Protectors He said that they were there to radiate God's Glory throughout the Earth. Alastair couldn't help but feel that they had lost the truth about God in their history. Just like the dragons had. His thoughts began to wander about how He could reveal the truth of God to them. Then he remembered that dragons and humans didn't get along so well. So how was that going to work out for either of them? He knew he was going to have to think about this for a while.

God's Presence filled the cave and it was like there was a warm, cozy fire in the cave with me. All my feelings of shame and hurt melted away. My mind cleared and I was at peace. I hadn't been that peaceful- ever. I drifted off to sleep. A deep sleep. I am Alastair and I was never going to be who my father wanted me to be.   I was called to the Light.

Chapter Three: Alexander

3

Alastair read the testimonies of the great dragons who served on the League of Protectors. To this day he would read all the books he could gather. Both in fable, folklore, and real testimonies. He has read great accounts of people who have said that Alexander was a muscular, strong dragon. He was tall like his father was. His scales were hard as stone and were dark teal with gold thinned at the edges. His tail was broad and his scales continued down along the top of his spine. His horns were long and went straight up beside his face in between his ears. Alexander's eyes were light gray and he carried a strength in his face just like his father did. Alexander came from a long line of distinguished dragons who were chosen by God to serve on the League of Protectors. His father always told him and his brothers stories of the great acts of the dragons who served on The League of Protectors. Their family always excelled right to the top of any group. His grandfather, his father, and Alexander's brothers were also chosen to serve. When he grew up he wanted to be just like them. He came from a supportive, attentive father and a loving, doting mother. He even had his older brothers teach and correct all his mistakes. He knew the correct answer to any problem that could arise against the guard and how to deal with it. Alexander never knew what it meant to be alone. He was always surrounded by support, love, and unfortunately, a great cloud of witnesses waiting on him to fail. When Alexander was very young he learned he could see into the future. A characteristic of one of his gifts that was revealed when he was a young dragon. A gift that he has kept to himself. He felt like he was cheating at everything he did but he could look several minutes into the future and see events before they unfolded. He always knew how to take the next steps to keep the team safe. For this reason, he never felt like there was any danger. But he kept it a secret from his family, his friends, and even from God. Or so he thought he was.

Alexander was also especially gifted with organization and his resourcefulness to get things done swiftly. He efficiently took care of delegating tasks and making sure they were done exactly the way God wanted them done. Which enabled his gifts of administration to excel in his life when he became a protector. It made him the perfect choice to become the leader to keep order and peace with all the dragons. He was amazing at his responsibilities. The League of Protectors has been operating at the highest level of all the teams of protectors that came before them because of Alexander and his gifts. The Heavens were organized, clean, and operating with such peace and delightfulness that had never experienced before. He always would say, "Clean area, clean mind." He often would tell you that if you were feeling like everything in your life was in chaos and disarray then it was more than likely your spirit man needing to spend some time cleaning the house. Spiritually and physically.

He also carried the Gift of Prophecy. A gift that allowed him to see a little into the future. A very rare gift that had manifested itself in the most peculiar way. No dragon has ever been said to have had this gift before Alexander. This was the gift that he was made aware of when he was younger. A gift that manifested earlier than most other dragons. Most dragons don't start to see signs of their gifts till they are hitting their teen years and have a lot of hormonal changes when they are coming of age. But in Alexander, he had to grow up a little earlier than most other dragons and so his gifts manifested earlier. These were the tales that he read in fables and stories, but there was always made-up fiction in fables but there was always some truth as well.

His testimony says that when Alexander was younger he was outside playing with some of his friends racing to see who was the fastest at flying through the trees. They had set up an obstacle course with booby traps and things to pop out to scare you and distract you from getting to the finish line first. Alexander took off and when the first trap went off and scared him, his vision changed. He was further ahead in the race than where he was when the trap went off and it felt different. He was higher up, looking down on the race as if he was no longer in the race but observing the race from up the air. Everything had a haziness, almost a slight glow to it. It appeared to be a dreamlike state that he was in. He saw himself pass by and he saw every mistake that he made. Then in an instant, he was back to the very first trap that went off and everything was in real color and in the present time again. He proceeded to finish the race, only this time he finished without making the mistakes that he had made in the dream. After a fun-filled day with his friends, he went home and all he could think about was his daydream. What happened to him that made him see that? Was it something he did? If it was how could he do it again?

Alexander spent the next few days trying to replicate what had happened. It was hard to do because he was in a race and the only thing that he could remember that could have caused the vision to come was that he got scared and he jumped when the first trap went off. So how was he supposed to replicate getting scared again when he was all alone in the woods? Was that the only trigger? Because he doesn't want to have to be surprised every time he wants to see the future again. There had to be a better way to activate the process. It was driving him crazy. Everything he tried wasn't working. He gave it all the time he had for the day. Of course, he was only seven. So time wasn't something he wanted to afford. Kids in the neighborhood could wait on no one. So off into the woods, he went. Maybe, if he was lucky, something would happen that would help him uncover the mystery for him. However, right now there was nothing more important than beating everyone else back into the woods to the fort they had built next to the mountain.

The fort was something they built where a young dragon kid could fantasize and could come to life. Today they had planned to take out an evil monster that was attacking the castle. They were supposed to meet at the fort to plan their defenses. There were only three of them and they had to be ready to take on the monster. He wasn't sure yet who would take the lead but he knew one thing was for sure. That monster was going to come at them with full force and they had to be ready. Their first plan was to create an obstacle that would help their speed get faster. Then they were going to build a monster look alike so they could plan their physical attack. He was excited to get started and he was getting anxious for them to get there.

Alexander was the first to arrive. He went in and sat down in the fort. He began to tidy up the fort and put things where they were supposed to go. He grabbed the broom and started to sweep the floor. Looking around he began to feel his loneliness. Alexander couldn't help but wonder where everyone was at. He got tired of sitting inside the fort and waiting, so he went out to walk the perimeter to wait for the others to get there. He went ahead and got started gathering materials for the obstacle course and the stuff for the traps. Several hours went by and no one showed. Alexander began to feel uncomfortable. He could sense that there was something wrong. The dark rain clouds closed in on him and he knew he had to fly home. He took a big deep breath in and opened his wings to take flight. He was only seven, so his parents told him that he always had to fly below the tree cover to keep him from attracting larger flying animals that might seek him as prey. So through the trees, he flew as fast as he could. Dodging limbs and avoiding branches that sought to take him out. He could feel his heart racing. Something was wrong. For a while, he flew along the river banks to avoid the trees and be able to fly faster without distraction from his speed. The closer he got to his home the anxiety increased.

He rounded the small hill where the trees opened up near his cave. Something didn't feel right. So he landed and hid behind a group of trees and brush and looked at the cave opening. There was always a small pillar of smoke that came out of the mouth of the cave and curled around the top of the opening, disappearing into the clouds. His mother always had a fire lit to keep the cave warm for his family. Without a fire lit, the rocks in the cave would be too cold to the touch and painful to lay on. He was thankful for his mother who kept their cave so warm. It was her touch that made all her sons feel like they could take on the world. She was their source of strength. She pulled them all together and made them behave like a family. They could be in the worst fight of their lives with each other over something not worth fighting over and all she had to do was call them inside and make them talk. She had a way of knowing exactly what to do or say to make everything right again.

She was the caregiver but their father was always the protector. If there was ever trouble with one of the boys, he was the one to swoop in and defend them. He was mighty and very strong. He towered over any opponent that would cross his path. One time when Alexander's brother was out on a hunt for food he came face to face with a gigantic black bear. The bear was a momma bear and she was only protecting her cubs from the mean dragon trying to eat them. However, she was more than Ezekiel could handle. He got too close to her and she struck him with her claw and knocked him off his feet. Ezekiel yelped in fear. Their father must have been nearby watching over Ezekiel during his hunt because he flew in without any hesitation and with his mighty snout picked her up and tossed her in the air away from his son. Alexander's older brother, Ezekiel was always the older brother who had to watch over Alexander when their parents went out on their own to hunt alone.

One time he took Alexander to the river to throw rocks and make the water splash to kill some time. They spent the afternoon enjoying the warmth of the sun and the time in the water. Nothing was better than some free time to splash and play with your older brother. When Alexander got a little tired from playing in the deep part of the river, the sat on the side of the riverbank and looked at the different sizes of rocks there were. Alexander loved looking at all the cool shapes and picking his favorite ones to take home to play with and remember the day with Ezekiel. They came across one that looked like an arrowhead. It was chiseled and sharp on one end and broken away for the other end of the rock to be fastened to a stick for people to use as a weapon. His brother taught him all about the different ways people would use stuff from the woods to make weapons to hurt others or animals. It was a perfect end to a perfect day.

Ezekiel had left that morning to track a big bear family. He told his father he was going to scout out the route for the hunt later and then make his way safely back to the cave. However, it took him longer than expected to find the bear's cave. It turned out it wasn't a bear family at all. It was a human tracking team. They had placed bear blood all the way to the bottom of the region. Their father was always there and he was always the mysterious force protecting them and keeping them safe. He always made sure they had food in their cave to eat and that the cave was safe from evil and darkness.

His mother and father made their home a good home. But there was no smoke rising when Alexander got to the opening of the cave. The cave was dark without her fire burning. There were signs that there had been a struggle on the cave walls. A flash of dragon's fire embossed the cave rock of one of their attackers. Several human bodies were lying on the ground. When Alexander left to go play with his friends, his mother and father were still in the caving curled up together by the fire where they slept. He had two other brothers that were older than him. Chase had left the cave a few days earlier, but Alexander did not know why. Ezekiel left around the same time he did to go on a hunt for food. There was no sign that he had returned home. None of Alexander's family was there. Alexander walked around the cave, looking for a sign that would tell him where his parents were. He stepped out of the stoop of the cave and looked for his family but they were nowhere in sight. The dark clouds finally came and brought a thunderous rain down upon him. Alexander didn't know what to do. He had nowhere to go. He curled up on the cold stone floor of the cave and cried himself to sleep. Hoping that they would come home any minute and this would be a horrible bad dream.

God could never understand why when given the choice to master their human lives, humans would always choose to hurt others to get ahead. When man was poor they would steal. When man was hungry for companionship they would take their women. When they didn't like their station in life they would kill some innocent creature to appeal to the people higher up the food chain than them. With humans, it was always about power over another life. So when Alexander's parents were taken from their cave His heart was broken for Alexander. God could only see the devastation it left behind for the ones it hurt so deeply. For Alexander, the pain was almost too much to bear. When Alexander woke up in the cave, he didn't know what to do next. He was always awakened by one of his parents to get up and get ready for the day, but today he was stirred awake by the cold wind blowing through the cave. Since his mother's fire was no longer burning the rock had turned cold and the wind was now bellowing through him. He never realized how much the fire pushed the cold out of their home till now. With his family gone, he was lost. He was only seven and he felt incapable of going on a big rescue mission to save them. If his parents couldn't overcome the humans, how was he supposed to?

Normally his mother would have his breakfast ready for him to eat.

Normally. But today he just wasn't hungry for anything. At first, Alexander was sad and depressed but the more he thought about his parents being taken from him for their horns, claws, and scales he became furious with anger and rage. What gave humans the right to hurt us this way? He and his family never did anything to them. They lived high up on the mountain and never went down into the valley where the town's people lived. They only ate wild deer and animals in the forest. So why would they need to bother his family? Alexander could no longer stand by and do nothing about it. He needed to do something to find his family. But he wasn't old enough yet to spit fire and he had just learned how to fly fast through the trees. He decided that when it became dark, he was going to fly down to the town and see if he could find out about his parents and brother.

~ * ~

The day was moving slowly and he couldn't wait for the darkness to come over the land so that he could go down the cliffs and see if he could find his family. But it was still morning and his impatience was getting the best of him. Staring out over the fields below the mouth of the cave he could hear his older brother Chase now lecturing him. "Alex, sit still and be patient. The deer will come out shortly after the rain has stopped. You can't expect the deer to come running out into the field for food in the middle of a severe thunderstorm!" Alexander has always been an impatient dragon. He wished he could hear his brother's voice sitting with him right now. He wished he could hear his love and guidance as he waited to go to search for his parents. He felt so alone. He was all alone for the first time in his life. No one to tell him what to do or what to say. No one to impress or disappoint. There was no one there to tell him how to rescue his mother and father.

The sun moved across the sky like it was a snail trying to get to the other side of the field. It was mid-day and although the sun was right above him he would've never known if it weren't for his stomach growling so loudly. But he didn't feel like he was safe to go out in the forest and hunt. What if there were people out there looking for more dragons? If his mother and father couldn't escape from them how could he get away if they would try to capture him too? Alexander didn't want to risk it. But he knew that he had to eat something soon or his stomach would let him know all about it. Normally he would be out and about the forest with his friends and they would hunt together for their lunch. But today was different than any other day. All he could think about was the deer running through the fields behind the mountain. Or the rabbits and squirrels in the forest where they would play in their fort. His stomach was winning the argument that he was having with his mind.

Alexander's mind began plotting a safe and secure way for him to get to the fort where he could easily hide and hunt for food. He would quietly fall off the cliff's edge and fall to the grounds below after spending some time scouting the forest below to be sure that it was safe for him to leave. Human's eyes could not see as far away as a dragon's eyes could. So he felt he would be able to see them before they would see him. He scouted the forest for as long as he could. For as long as his stomach would allow. The sun was shining bright and the trees below were blowing in the summer's breeze. Now was as good a time as any. He crawled to the edge of the cliff and looked over the side. He was a little too close than he should have been. A few rocks shuffled their way off the edge falling to the trees below him. Alexander took a deep breath and stepped off the edge of the cliff.

Twisting in the wind as he fell to the ground snout first. His body was a small bullet piercing through the air. He lifted his head at the last possible second and opened his wings to aid him in guiding him to the forest floor. He followed his father's instructions and stayed as low to the ground as he could to remain out of sight from the predators above but he wasn't sure how he was supposed to secure himself against those predators that were on the ground with him. The only thing he knew how to do well was to hide behind the trees and brush the best that he could as he hunted for his lunch. It didn't take him long to find the food he needed. Thankfully because he was anxious to get back to the cave and continue to hide until the moon had risen. He was hesitant to go back to the cave. He didn't know why. Something in his heart was warning him to stay away from the cave. He fought these feelings for quite some time. He decided to sit in the fort for a while. So he could think about what to do next.

The fort was made of tree branches, rocks, and leaf coverage that were leaned up against the side of the old oak tree in the field next to the mountain where his cave was. He wasn't too far away from the cave but he felt safer down here than he would be up there. He didn't know why he knew this was better. He just did. The next thing he knew, he was hearing voices coming down the path. He quickly ducked behind a large bush and crouched low to the ground. Unsure of whether he was in danger or not, he hid in the darkness of the shadowed trees and was as quiet as he could be. The voice he heard was human. Two men, a woman, and three small children walking. They were carrying baskets and from what Alexander could smell it smelled like warm apples but it had a different smell than he was used to. It smelled like home but he knew it was not. He opened his eyes and wouldn't allow his longing for his mother to cloud his mind from protecting himself now. He had to stay alert and be vigilant about his surroundings or he could easily put himself in grave danger. The humans kept walking by and as he watched them carefully he found himself wanting to get to know them. The mother was so delightful. Just like his mother was. The father played with the children and raced with them down the path. He couldn't understand how these people could be considered so dangerous to him. But he had to listen to his father's warnings. He was supposed to be on a mission to get back to the cave safely but his curiosity was getting the best of him. He continued to follow the family down the mountain and before he knew it he was on the edge of the woods just outside the town limits. There was a big building and it smelled like a field with dead long grass in it. He decided it was the best place for him to hide until it got darker and he could hide up in the loft area until then. Who knows maybe he will see his family. Although he longed to see them, he wished he could know more about the family of humans he was following.

~ * ~

The night crept in. The rain clouds came in slowly making everything wet and the ground soft. This worked well in Alexander's favor because the night sky covered in rain clouds made it considerably darker and the shadows longer. The darkness allowed Alexander to creep around town in the shadows to see if he could see or hear anything about his family that was taken from him. He started at the edge of the forest and worked his way around the backs of the buildings all through town. He made it to the docks where the boats were. He decided it would be best if he got down quietly into the water to search the boats better. He could hide his body in the waves coming into the land.

Ships were heading out into the seas as he swam around the docked ships. He could hear some of the one ship's crew talking in the galley inside one of the boats. He decided to swim closer to the boat. The window was ajar and allowed him to hear what they were saying. They were talking about some of the large creatures that were brought aboard one of the ships that sailed out earlier this morning. He said that the men who had to sail with them were not looking forward to the trip. It was not a good omen to transport such evil creatures from their habitat. The one guy said that the larger of the two had spit fire at them when he was being captured in his cave before they had shot him with a tranquilizer dart to put him to sleep. Thankfully they had already shot the other one with a dart before that one could make any fire. They didn't know how they made the fire but it wasn't safe to travel with them.

Alexander got excited because they were talking about his mother and father! Then he realized that they were talking about his mother and father being on a boat that sailed away from the town. He was too late to save them. He was too young to fly great distances over the ocean. Then it hit him. They only captured two dragons in the cave. That meant his two brothers were still here and they were alive and could help him. So he set on a journey to look for his brothers…

~ * ~

Alexander had grown into a mighty warrior. His stories have been passed down through the ages. From one generation to the next. The tales always come down to this last statement that can be made. "We don't know what led him to go along with Drake and his horrible plans to be greater than God." Parents can only end their story time with this warning. "You see, kids, evil can sneak in on you and before you know it, you're on the wrong side of history." After Alexander left the town where the humans lived and began his search for his brothers. However, he never found them. He searched everywhere. Chase and Ezekiel were nowhere to be found. Alexander was left to fend for himself. He no longer had anyone to care for him. All of a sudden his game with his friends seemed so trivial and childlike.

From that moment on Alexander set out to find his parents on his own. He spent the next several years chasing down leads to find out where his mother and father had been shipped off to. The ship had to have a destination it was sailing to and he was determined to find out where. Hiding in the shadows he lurked behind whatever he needed to to hear conversations involving his parents or other dragons who were captured by the same hunters. He learned a lot about why they were being hunted. Hunted for everything from their magical properties to the gold-scaled dust and ivory horns for humans to mount on their walls. Apparently, his parents were captured by a trade master who was called The Breeder. He was after all the dragons for their eggs. So capturing his parents together was an exceptional event. The Breeder was proud of himself and wanted to get his new dragons back to his castle to begin their breeding.

That was good news to Alexander. That means his parents were still alive. He was worried that they were being hunted for their skin or their claws. But since that was not the case, Alexander knew he had some time to get them out of captivity. Now all he had to do was find out exactly where they were being held so that when he could finally make the trip across the seas, he would know where to go. That frustrated Alexander because he did not know how long that would take. He kept trying to remember how old his mother said he was going to be when he could fly that far. But at the time he dismissed her argument. They were just talking about him growing older and faster at bedtime one night before bed. He didn't want to hear that it was going to take longer. He wanted to be as old as Ezekiel and Chase. They were already big enough to make long-distance trips and he thought it wasn't fair that he couldn't go with them. These memories were hard for him to remember not because of a bad memory but because they were times as a family. Together. All he had to worry about was whether or not he had brought enough sticks to the fort for a project or if he had drank enough water before he would have to go home in the evening. He wishes he could remember when his mother said that he would be old enough to fly that far, but he could not remember. The best he could recollect was that he knew how old his brothers were when they made their trip and that would have to do. Till then he spent his days strengthening his mind and body for the battle he was one day going to have to face.

~ * ~

Alexander never knew that his life was going to be changed so terribly. One day he had a loving family, a safe, warm home to go to. He had everything he could have ever wanted at seven years old. Older brothers to look up to. A father he revered and honored. A mother he loved and gave the best snuggles. He was now thirteen and he feels like it has been a lifetime of pain and heartache. Better described as a life of loneliness. He continued to spend his days training his body to fly further, go harder, and need less. In six years, he never realized that today would be the day he would leave his homeland to find his parents.

The day got started like any other day before it. He got up. Got something to eat. Then headed up into the mountains where he could be sure he wouldn't be spotted by humans. He always went deep into the valley where the cliffs and rocks were high up and hard to get to by foot. This way he would be free to fly for a very long time. He could continue to push himself each day and not have to worry about being seen. He could also go down into the trees and race in and out of the treetops to increase his cornering capabilities. Normally, he would do each of his exercises four times before he would stop training and eat lunch. But today he finished early. So he decided to head back closer to his cave. When he got down the mountain he decided to walk and rest his wings.

Lost in his thoughts as he walked along the forest floor, Alexander wondered how his family was doing. He never figured out what or where his two brothers went. Aside from training each day, he would observe humans and how they lived. He never had any contact with them no matter how much he wanted to. He could never trust how he felt about them and how they really would treat him was completely different. He always sided with that he should just be cautious. Especially since humans were always looking for new dragons to capture for a trader or a hunter. It was just better that he remain in the dark for now.

Every day when the night came across the cliffs Alexander would jump off the edge and fly as far as he could. At first, he would tire out easily and would have to fly back to land before he would make it anywhere too far away that he couldn't make it back to land. But today he was able to fly and his lungs didn't feel stressed like they had before. He flapped his wings and kept rising higher and higher. Getting further away from home. In his years of looking for his parents, he found out that he had to fly north to the land they called Baltica. He also found out that there was a third dragon captured the same day as his parents and that there was a third ship in the fleet. He knew it was going to be cold and there just was no way for him to prepare for the temperature changes that awaited him. He found out that The Breeder had a big castle on the furthest tip of the land before the land started to freeze into ice caps. He ate well before taking off so that he wouldn't have to worry about landing anywhere unsafe. He was finally doing it. He was finally able to make the flight. He had waited so many years to make this trip. His only regret was that he wished he was making it with one of his brothers. But he couldn't rest in those thoughts. They only saddened him. He had to remain positive. He had to encourage himself during his flight. He had to think about what he needed to be focused on. His trip and making the most miles that he could while it was dark because when the sunrise occurred his trip would have to come to an end to remain unseen. So into the darkness, he flew. Keeping the Northern Star of Baltica right in front of him. He took a deep breath and pushed onwards.

Chapter Four: Ziggy

4

Then there was Ziggy. He was a creature unlike any other. Slightly smaller than the rest of the dragons, but he was made that way on purpose. Ziggy was the protector of all the children and babies that came into Heaven. Like his name, Ziggy was very colorful; both in his personality and in his appearance. Ziggy's skin tone was a light sky blue color and when the sunlight hit his scales a vibrant spectrum of colors lifted into the air. Ziggy's appearance called the children just like their favorite stuffed animal would. Always full of hugs and silly facial expressions to make anyone laugh. He just had a playful way to make your day better.

Ziggy didn't look like the other dragons. He wasn't as big or as magnificent as his brothers and sisters in the League of Protectors. Not that he isn't as powerful, because he is. His powers came from a different place than the other dragons. His powers came from his experiences. His story isn't like theirs. When he was born he wasn't as strong, as cute, or as magical. He was born and there was no breath in him. He had no color and his scales were weak and brittle. His mother and father didn't see his worth. His father laid him in the woods next to the mountain. His mother leaned down and kissed him sweetly, and then they flew away. All that his parents could see was that he wasn't normal and that he might not make it through life. All they knew were the standards of what it was to be a perfect drake and since Ziggy didn't meet with those perfect ideologies he was discarded like last night's trash. Thrown to the mercy of the night on the mountainside. His parents thought he was better off feeding another creature than being their precious son. But God saw differently. He knew why He created Ziggy.

Although all the dragon protectors lived in heaven to protect the people they were not born there. Their lives all begin hatched on Earth and lived beside the people. They had to experience life for themselves. When God found them to be noble and righteous dragons they were then chosen to be part of the League of Protectors. There were only twelve stations that had the dragons placed to be His Protectors. There was no station for a dragon to protect the babies and the children. The twelve dragons each had a different purpose and function set forth since the beginning of time. So while on Earth, if a dragon followed the path that was laid before his or her feet, and listened to the Holy Spirit they would find their purpose for which God had created them. So when Ziggy's parents chose to leave Ziggy behind, God knew that Ziggy's life was worth far more than his parents could have ever envisioned. God knew he needed to be rescued and set on the correct path. God unfortunately also knew that it was the abandonment that would make Ziggy an amazing protector for God's Children that came home to Heaven. If Ziggy could learn to overcome the hurt and pain of being discarded by his parents and could overcome the obstacles his life had set before him.

God found Ziggy alone, whimpering, and crying under a full blackberry bush he had rolled under after his parents left him. God picked up Ziggy and calmed his cries. He nestled Ziggy in His arms and wrapped him in a blanket. Ziggy was still too young to create his inner fire. So a blanket was needed to keep him warm still. It was a good thing God was watching over him. God took Ziggy with Him and began to nourish his weak, cold body with the first warm milk from the herd. Once he got a little bit older and had teeth he could be released back into the mountainside to fend for himself. The Holy Spirit would guide and lead him to find his path to the Light. The Holy Spirit would unction all dragons to go towards the good and to stay away from evil ways but not every dragon listened. Every dragon had free will to listen and follow God's lead. It was their choice.

After God released Ziggy back to the forest, he spent a lot of time alone. He didn't have siblings, parents, or family to teach him how to pass the time. There wasn't someone to guide him to go get something to eat, or where there was a safe place to rest. The only company

Ziggy had was the hope for a better future with friends, games, and laughter. He had nature and his thoughts for the longest time. So it was only reasonable that Ziggy would come up with his games to keep him busy throughout the day. It was amazing how resourceful a pine cone could become when you're bored. Or how adventurous a deep cavern could be on a cold wintry night. Once Ziggy learned how to make fire with his spit, keeping warm at night wasn't as hard as it used to be. Ziggy would see other animals in the forest and he would see mothers and fathers caring for their young. Ziggy's mind would wander in his thoughts and that was a question he often wondered. He knew he was a dragon but he didn't know why he was the only one. He wished he had a family to love and care for him like the other animals did. At least that's what he thought about until he came across a rabbit's nest. He was going to make them his lunch until something told him to just watch them.

He watched these babies from up in a tree for hours. He watched them scurry about eating berries from the bushes and nuts from the forest floor. He thought that they were just like him. They had no family and no parents to teach them. But then he noticed a momma rabbit who would return twice a day and check in on them. Occasionally she would bring food or her milk to them, but for most of their day, she was away. Every time she was near Ziggy would smell her coming. She carried a heavy scent and he concluded that she was going away to protect them till they were old enough to be on their own. Ziggy concluded that some animals didn't care for their young as he had imagined. All animals were different. Including Ziggy. So maybe a dragon was like a rabbit and the mother and father would go away to protect them. However, that logic didn't last too long because he never saw any other dragons.

When Ziggy realized he was a different kind of animal, he somehow felt secure in who he was. He may never know who his parents were, but he figured that he must be like the rabbits. Only loved for a little while and then released into the world to discover and play. So that's exactly what Ziggy did; every day. He would make a game or a mystery out of his surroundings and since he was a dragon and could live wherever he wanted, then his surroundings were constantly changing every day. He loved the days when he was close to a large lake or by the sea. He loved playing in the water and the sand. He could build sand castles as big as he was and crawl through them. Or he could make caves out of the sand and crawl in them for the coolness the deep sand would provide. His imagination was amazing at telling stories and keeping him entertained for hours.

At least on most days, he could keep his mind busy. Most days. Today, for some reason was different. Today he just didn't feel like re-enacting a story or creating a family out of twigs and rocks. He woke up and the clouds felt like they were closer and darker than any other day. He began to wonder what the point of his life was. Was this all he was ever going to do? Get up, eat, play, eat, play, go to sleep…Every day? There had to be more. There had to be other dragons out there. He couldn't be the only one. What was the point of being able to talk if you had no one to talk to? What was the point of loving to play and create if there was no one to share it with?

~ * ~

When Ziggy got older he flourished in caring for the animals in the forest that were young and separated from someone else to protect and care for them. He was a natural caregiver despite never having someone to look up to for his care. He always took the best care and loved after those who needed it the most. If they were injured he would make bandages and care for their wounds until they were better and could make it on their own again. For a dragon who has never felt the warmth of a mother's love, he sure did know how to love others well. However, he never knew what it felt like to be loved so how did he know how to be the example of something he had never had? Everywhere he went he attracted those who needed to be held, cared for, and loved. Without any hesitation, Ziggy gave the best hugs, the warmest smiles, and the most heartfelt well wishes that could ever be given.

Ziggy was almost fifteen years old this month and he planned to do something that he had never done before. For himself, for his birthday. He decided he wanted to build a house in the cave he came across when he flew into this area. There were a lot of animals that could use his help and he felt like it was time for him to stay somewhere permanently and make himself a home. There was an underground cavern near the waterfalls. He was going to go and look them over a little later today when he was finished up with some of his new friends who needed his help. Which wouldn't be too long because he was anxious to get settled into his new home. He had never had one before. A home. He just always moved to and from places and lay wherever it was convenient and safe for him to lay his head at night. So when he landed here he felt like this was as good a place as any for him to make his home. He had a place to live, some animals needed him, and he liked the surrounding areas. Once he looked over the cave by the waterfalls and once he felt that they were okay. He would begin to make this new area his new home.

There were steep mountain cliff ranges in the area that made it hard for people to get there on foot. So he felt pretty comfortable that those mountain ranges would be a perfect place to fly and hunt without worrying about humans. Many goats, bears, and deer were in those hills so food wouldn't be an issue. The waterfalls would be a perfect place for him to hide at night behind the curtain of water falling. He didn't see any other large flying predators that he would need to worry about. So all in all he thought this was a perfect place to call his home. All afternoon as he was helping other animals all he could think about was flying over to the cave and seeing what the inside looked like. The outside when he flew over several times looked pleasant. The day was a little dark and cloudy. So he was anxious to see what it looked like in the sunlight. The river above was rather wide and it cascaded down the mountain rocks vigorously. The mouth of the cave was hidden beautifully by tree vines and lush flowering morning glory wildflowers. The fall's rocks were moist with moss and greenery. A perfect landscape for him to get nutrient-rich bandages for his friends in need. The moss is a perfect aid in helping fur and skin heal from a burn from a fire. Something a young dragon learns all too quickly how to heal from.

He hoped the inside caves ran deep into the mountain. Giving him plenty of coverage from people and other animals who might venture their way into the cave. He could hide further in the cave where his eyes would adapt and see in the darkness without light. Many other animals could not see once it got so dark. But a dragon's eyes could see anything without any light at all. A trait that would later unveil itself more to him when Ziggy gets a lot older. But he only knew what today's adventures could bestow. Before Ziggy knew it, there were no more friends to help and he was finally free to go look at the cave.

~ * ~

The afternoon clouds looked full and ready to break open at any minute. The winds had picked up slightly creating a cool summer breeze in the afternoon air. The stalks of corn growing in the fields near the farmer's family home were curled pointing straight into the sky; begging the Lord for rain. Ziggy flew high in the cloud's coverage to keep clear of being seen by anyone. He was not aware that people were living this far out in the country away from the town. As Ziggy flew over their home he could see smoke coming out of the smokestack and small children were playing in the grass in a tent made of a thin sheet of linen. It was a pleasant picture that made Ziggy long to know more about them. But today was not that day. Today was all about his new home in the cave.

As he approached the waterfalls, several white-tailed deer were eating lush green grass near the bottom of the falls. They sensed Ziggy coming near and jumped up to run for cover the moment he came into sight. Ziggy landed on the green grass right beside them and bowed his head to show them he meant them no harm. The mother deer bowed her head in response then nestled her young to make their way out of the area. She was no longer frightened of Ziggy but she did not want to tempt their fate if she were wrong. Ziggy stayed still with his head down till she was away and she felt safe again. He was used to other animals' fear. It did not bother him any longer. He taught himself it was better to just be a gentleman about the matter. Only time could give him the relationship with the animals that he longed for. One built with trust and hope for a future with them working together for the greater good. Until then he just had to be patient and wait till that day could arrive.

He looked around the falls and it was just as he had remembered. The thick cover of trees around the river above and surrounding the pool of water below was perfect for him. The shadows that trees created were a safety that all dragons knew too well. The shadows provided them with a secret spot in the forest that kept them from harm. Ziggy learned how to hide from the other animals in the forest when he was growing up. People were not an unfamiliar danger in the forest but the smaller animals showed Ziggy that they didn't always have to run out in the open to get away from them. They showed him that they could just hide in the darkness until the humans gave up and went on about their way in search of a bigger animal. Ziggy was used to being in the dark shadows. He felt safe there.

Ziggy spread open his wings and flew up to the opening of the caves in the mountainside. The water that was falling was a thick blanket covering the mouth of the cave. That excited Ziggy. That meant that the caves were dark inside and would give him the safety he wished for in his home. The opening was a jagged hole. Sharp with breaks of limestone and slick with a moss-like film from the water in the falls. Ziggy pushed through the water to unveil the inside. As soon as his eyes adjusted, Ziggy could see that the cave was indeed large with hollowed-out rooms deep into the mountain. He could imagine a fire burning deep in the cave to provide warmth. He wished that he could imagine a female dragon to fall in love with to have little dragons running through this large cave. Calling this their home. Calling out to them, "Mother! Father!" He could see them all safe and protected from harm. He could see them all happy and loved. He wasn't sure if there was such a reality with a female dragon that would love him. He didn't know if she existed. Maybe only in his dreams. But he could pray.

~ * ~

Ziggy has only ever had hope to look forward to. It's the only thing that has kept a future in his life. He has always carried the hope that in his future there will be a family. That there was someone out there who would love him and who missed him. Someone who never wanted to be away from him. There was always hope that he would no longer be alone and without a point to his life. He had a hope that in the future he would one day have everything he never had when he was growing up. Love, joy, peace. Hope gave him all those things.

He took a few steps to exit the cave and he heard voices. He got close to the curtain of water hoping to see outside. There were humans down by the pool of water. He could see their shapes but no details about them. The best he could see they were filling containers on their horses full of the pool's water and reattaching the containers to the seats. He wasn't sure how long they were going to be there so he sat down a little deeper in the cave, just in case they decided to come inside. He wished that this was already set up as his home because the floor wouldn't be so cold right now. He had forgotten how cold stone could be in the caves. He breathed deeply in his front claws. His breath was warm because of his inner fire. It could warm his claws long enough to wait out the humans below. He sat patiently waiting for time to pass by so that he could be on his way. He listened closely to them below as they played by the pool and talked about their plans for tomorrow.

Ziggy was always fascinated by humans and their ability to have hope for a better tomorrow for their family. Every time he witnessed humans in their lives they were always plotting and planning how they were going to get things done. It amused him. He watched as the children begged to play in the water as their parents hurried them to get their toys together so they could be on their way home. He assumed that these were the humans that belonged to the home he flew over on the way to the cave. The mother called out her son's name. Over and over as if he were lost. The men started shouting as well. A small shadow appeared at the mouth of the cave behind the water falling from above. The figure put his arms up on his head as if he were trying to cover his eyes from the sun to see inside the cave. Ziggy panicked. Worried that the child would walk through the water and come inside to explore on his own. Ziggy went deeper into the cave, just in case.

Good thing Ziggy did because the next thing he knew the boy pushed through the curtain of water and appeared in the cave. The water washed over him from head to toe. Soaking his whole body. His hair was a little long and it came down into his eyes with the water. The young boy threw up his hands to brush his hair and the water away from his eyes. He shook his head like a dog riding itself of its bath water. His eyes were adjusting to the darkness and so he stood still for a moment. Ziggy, was already acclimated to the dark, so he slowly moved in behind a big pile of rocks out of the boy's point of view. He may have been deep in the cave and the darkness safety, but Ziggy worried it wouldn't be enough and he'd be seen.

"Aaron? Aaron! Where are you?" His mother called out his name. We could hear the panic in her voice from the cave. The little boy knew she was worried too because he went to the mouth of the cave and called down to her to ease her screams. It only made things worse because she screamed louder for him to climb down from the rocks and the waterfalls. He was disappointed because he wanted to explore the cave more, but he knew his mother wasn't going to allow that to happen. So he would have to put off the exploration for another day when he could come here on his own and find out if there were any treasures. Aaron turned and looked back into the cave and Ziggy could see the longing on his face. Aaron's mother screamed his name several more times before he finally broke the temptation to stay and ran out of the mouth of the cave. "I'm coming, Mom!" he cried out and climbed down the rocks.

Ziggy sat down and took a big deep breath. That was close. Too close for his comfort. He had always stayed clear of being seen by any humans. So that was pretty close for Ziggy. There were only feet from each other and Ziggy could have been discovered easily if the boy was left alone to look around. His mother was pretty upset with him for climbing up there so it didn't seem like he would ever be back to bother Ziggy, However, Ziggy was a little unsettled about living there now because of his curiosity. He wasn't sure that he was safe anymore there. He decided not to panic too much but to be cautious and aware of his surroundings until he knew the cave was safe from any more people.

~ * ~

Aaron went home with his family like he was supposed to but he couldn't help but wonder what was inside the cave. He planned on going back there the first chance he could get. Most days were full of helping out with the chores that he had to do on the farm but on Saturday he was free to do whatever he wanted. Normally he would ride his bike and meet his friends in town at the ice cream shop or at the old feed stand that was closed now. He'd gather with friends and they would decide what they were going to do all day. Most days in the summer all they ever wanted to do was play in the river. In the hot summer's heat that's all anyone wanted to do. Stay hydrated and keep cool. But now all Aaron could think about was that cave. He lay in his bed remembering.

Aaron's mind always had a way of taking a tiny amount of detail and turning it into an elaborate ordeal. He always had a strong-willed spirit about him but his mother says that he gets to be a bit much sometimes. He would see a line of ants marching their way through the kitchen floor and Aaron had created some magnificent tale of their adventures getting around the hand towel he had placed in their way. It was all his Uncle Richard's doing. He was a traveling archaeologist and he would bring some pretty strange gifts and books when he visited them. There was always some crazy tale that accompanied the gift about lost treasures or missing people. It fueled Aaron's imagination for the adventures life had to offer him. But unfortunately for Aaron's mother, his curiosity always had some portion to play in prolonging the events. When most kids would see danger and run in the opposite direction, Aaron would run into the line of fire because there was something or someone who needed his help. He tossed and he turned trying to go to sleep but he couldn't stop thinking about what could be in that cave. He started to think about what the cave felt like when he went inside. Something was in there with him. He was not alone.

Inside the darkness of the cave, it was cooler than the outside only a few feet away. He could smell the dank air that came up from the depths of the cave. It smelled a lot like boiled eggs. The rocks were different colors, shapes, and sizes. Mineral formations were coming down from the ceiling of the cave and up from the floor of the cave. It was very dark in there. When he was gathering things for Saturday to come back and explore on his own he would have to remember to take a stick with rags on the end with gas to lite for a fire to see better. He was also going to have to remember to dress in clothes and shoes that were better for cave exploring. Shorts and a dress shirt like he wore today would never work. He knew that he was going to be getting dirty there. He fell asleep making plans for his adventures on Saturday. His dreams took him into more wild fantasies but his mind wasn't prepared for who he'd meet in a few days.

Aaron was just like Richard was when he was younger. Always on a plot to help take over the world or to save a damsel in distress. Richard saw himself in Aaron. Although he could see the likeness in Aaron, Richard also knew deep in his gut that Aaron's life was going to lead to something more fantastic. There was a sparkle in Aaron's eyes that glowed when he told his uncle about what he envisioned his future to be. He was always the hero in the tale and there was always a race of people that needed to be saved from some evil monster that only Aaron could see. All Richard hoped to ever do was to encourage his greatness. Something Richard often wished he'd had for himself when he was growing up. He felt like there was so much the world had to offer someone willing to go and get it. It was later in Richard's life when he realized he could achieve greatness. He didn't want Aaron and his sister to wait that long. So he inspired them the best that he could when he was around them.

~ * ~

Ziggy couldn't help but wonder whether his new cave was safe now. Since the young boy knew there was a cave behind the waterfalls. However, the boy didn't scare Ziggy. He was young and adventurous. He was just exploring his surroundings. What if Aaron came back to the cave and saw Ziggy? What would Ziggy do? What was Ziggy's plan if he was found? Captured? Maybe he should just find another place that was less trouble. Maybe he should move away from here altogether. But what if no one ever comes back to the pool or cave ever again? What if he was just jumping to conclusions and there was nothing to be worried about now that they were gone? Again, Ziggy took a deep breath and decided it was best to think about it tomorrow. For now, he would just sleep in the middle of the tall grass in the field next to the mountain. He had been sleeping there the last several nights and he felt it was best to stick to what was safe right now. Tomorrow Ziggy planned on sneaking by the old house to see if he could see if Aaron and his family lived in that house or if they were just travelers who had stopped by the waterfalls for water and rest. If that was the case, there was nothing to be worried about. Aaron and his family were just traveling through the area and the cave was safe. However, if Aaron lived in the farmhouse nearby then Ziggy might need to rethink his plans to move to the cave.

Ziggy was anxious to find out more, Staying asleep was proving to be very difficult for him this morning. After much tossing and turning in the grass once the sun was up, he decided he was just wasting his time. He got up and sought after his breakfast then started in the direction of the house. The sun was out bright and there was no safe cloud coverage for Ziggy to fly there. So he had to walk around through the dark shadows of the forest. It would take him a lot longer to get there but it was the only way he could make it to the farmhouse without being discovered or captured. The forest always felt like a safe place for Ziggy. Of course what dragon wouldn't like a forest that was full of berries and fruit trees?

He hadn't made it too far through the forest before he heard some commotion on the path. Ziggy lowered close to the ground behind some bushes. He waited but no one ever came down the path. He had heard a scream, then a noise that sounded like a clasping metal trap. Then there was a faint whimpering sound then silence. It all sounded a bit strange to Ziggy but for a dragon, it was always better to be safe and hide than be sorry and have to fight off a larger animal or a group of humans. Ziggy waited and the path still hadn't provided an answer to what in the world was going on. Ziggy decided to find out for himself this time.

He crouched low and inched towards the noise. He rounded the corner of the path and saw drag marks leading off the path into the woods. As he got to the marks and could see where they led, his eyes had to be deceiving his mind. There on the ground lay a human man and a boy leaned over him trying to wake him. As soon as his eyes saw them, Ziggy crouched back into the darkness of the trees nearby. The boy got up and kept telling his dad he needed to wake up and tell him what to do. It was Aaron and his father. His father was caught in one of the steel hunter's traps. The pain was too much and his father passed out. Aaron was by himself and was frightened. Ziggy was faced with an awful decision. Reveal himself to Aaron and help them out. Or stay out of it and let fate continue its course? Whatever the universe would decide.

Chapter Five: Angelina

5

Last but not least, we are left with Angelina. One of the four female dragons ever chosen to serve in the League of Protectors. In our bloodline, there have only been four females selected. Being chosen to serve in the League was a great achievement, but to be a female dragon to serve was truly an honor. All her league brothers and sisters loved Angelina. Which was quite a feat in itself because there were many. She never started conflict and when it was needed she was always the one who stood up to stop it. She was a peacekeeper. There always seemed to be a mystery about her. Never loud or outgoing. Just quiet and to herself. Independent and strong. Stronger than she looks. Angelina has always had increased strength despite her small female physique.

She was born on Earth just like other dragons in her time. However, her birth was anything but normal. Her mother was already overwhelmed by her two brothers and so when she came along, she was more than her mother could handle. Her father was gone. He left them when he found out his mother was pregnant with her. He was never around to help her as he was with her brothers. Her mother was devastated when her father left. Her brothers were already old enough to kind of care for themselves but Angelina had no one looking after her. So as a baby, she cried a lot because she needed her momma to feed her. But her mother was not there. Thankfully she only needed milk from her mother for a few months when her teeth came in and she could eat small animals for food. Angelina started to learn early that she had no one she could rely on to meet her needs. That was the case for both physical and emotional needs. Her mother became very bitter and angry with life. So there were very few cuddly moments with her only daughter. Which became the normal day for Angelina.

When Angelina was very young, she was on an outing with her mother, her brothers, and some other friends setting fire to a field and a farm for warmth on a cold winter's day. They all lay down when the fire was at its fullest to get a good night's sleep. She did not want to lie down in the same place as her brothers, so she went a little further away beside a tree trunk and slept. When she woke up early the following day, she saw she was alone. Her parents, her brothers, and all of their friends were gone. She looked and flew around for hours searching for them. She concluded that they had left in the night and were not aware that she was not with them. This has happened a few times in her life. They always wondered why she thought she was invisible to them. But how could she not feel this way when they did things like this to her? Although, the other times when they had forgotten her they eventually came back to where they last were and gathered her up. Complaining that it was her fault for not paying attention to them and being more observant of her surroundings. She wondered how they were going to blame her for this. She was asleep. But hours went by and she never left the area, just in case they returned enraged that they had to come back looking for her. They never came. Days turned into weeks. Weeks turned into months. She finally concluded that they were never coming for her. She was alone. At fourteen years old, she began to feed and care for herself on her own. After a while, she got used to the quiet.

Angelina became stronger and more independent as she got older. She had crossed paths with other dragon families who would try to take her in and care for her but she liked being alone. She didn't have to worry about whether she was doing something right or wrong according to them. She didn't have to worry about caring for anyone else but herself. Of course, that also meant that she would never get hurt if they didn't want to be with her any longer. She never had to worry about the hurt and pain the rejection would cause if they left. It was better this way for everyone. Especially her.

Angelina always felt that she was invisible when she was growing up. She never stood out in a crowd and she always had to speak up in her family to be heard. She was often overlooked and underestimated at every moment. So much so that her skin eventually began to change and developed into something new along with her abilities. Now when she feels like she's not there, when she feels invisible to others, her skin changes to blend into her background. Sort of like a chameleon does when they feel threatened. Her body adjusts to her surroundings and gives the illusion that she is not there. Or at least that is what she thought was happening. However, in Angelina's case, she found out that when she feels like she's blended into her background she isn't there anymore. When Angelina fades out of our view she disappears to another place. Angelina can move in and out of the spirit realm. Fading her existence leaving Earth's realm and entering the realm where only spirits live.

God used to walk with the first people in the cool of the evening. Now, He can barely get them to say His name without anger and hate motivating them. To humans, God has been diminished to a myth or a legend. Which is sad, because God has only wanted what was best for them the whole time. Angelina found God in the spirit realm. In her despair, she was only trying to disappear from a black bear in the forest, and as she closed her eyes to blend into the trees she turned to realize she was no longer in the forest. She was standing in a dark cave looking outside at the mouth of the cave to the sky. She took a few steps toward the opening and she realized she was not alone. She stood very still and began to look around the cave to see if she could see who she felt was with her.

As she turned her neck to the right, she saw light appear out of the darkness. Starting as a pinpoint of light it grew into a large, melon-sized glowing ball of radiating blue light. From this orb, a male voice spoke to her. "Good Morning, Angelina." She didn't know what to say or to do. She was surprised but not afraid. She felt at peace hearing His voice. She knew in her heart that she should be humbled and she laid down on the floor before Him. She replied to the orb. Not exactly sure if it had a name or how to address the talking blue light. "Good Morning, Sir." He spoke again. "It has been a while since anyone has come to talk with me." She couldn't help herself. She giggled under her breath and asked, "You. Might I know who you are? Do you have a name?" His reply will forever be written in her heart for the rest of her life. "I am the Alpha and the Omega. I am the beginning and the End. I am Jehovah Jireh. I am He."

Some people throughout history have held spiritual powers that would allow them to project into the spirit realm to communicate to the Holy Spirit for wisdom, guidance, and instructions. Humans have always found great comfort when talking with the Holy Spirit in person. There is always such a feeling of peace and reverence in His Presence. All they had to do was go into their quiet, secret place and call on God to be with them. The Holy Spirit would come and fill the room. Hours would feel like just minutes. In His Presence, hearts would be changed, burdens would disappear, and direction would be clear. There was no experience like being in the Presence of God. It wasn't something that could be faked. You went into a place and before you knew it He would help you understand what was troubling you so badly. He would help you get rid of the mountain that was in your way. Whether He would take the burden off your mind or He would show you how to let it go, but when you left His Presence it was no longer with you. Or your perspective about the matter would be forever changed. Regardless, it was an amazing experience.

However, over time people have lost their need for God. They no longer depend on Him like they used to. So calling on Him has become a lost art for only spiritual leaders; priests or prophets. But one thing all people who follow after God know is that He is never done with transforming you into a better version of yourself. So when Angelina was in the Spirit realm with God talking and learning from Him she couldn't help but see the errors in our ways. God would reveal Himself to her and show her a different facet of His being and when she would come out she would see the problems that needed to be resolved not only within herself but in the humans as well. His guidance would become vital in the days ahead but right now God just needed her to see Him and who He was. So that when things would get more challenging in the future she could walk through the fears she would ultimately have to face.

Until that day, she never knew anything about God. She wasn't raised with parents who told her anything about Him. The only thing they ever taught her was that she wasn't worthy and that she was a burden they wished they could be rid of. However, since then, Angelina has not gone one day without going to the spirit realm and talking with God. Through God, she has learned so much about life. He has taught her some amazing things about herself and who she is to Him. She never knew how important she was to Him. She learned that He has been calling her to Him her whole life. When she would feel a nudge to go toward a lighted flight pattern; that was Him. When she would feel like helping another younger dragon to keep warm at night; that was Him. When she felt warm for doing something kind or good; that was Him. He was always there leading her to the Light. After several months, He told her that He would have to go back to the Heavens. But He wanted her to know that the Holy Spirit was going to be there to help her along the way in her future. All she had to do was to call on His Name. Although she was saddened, she understood and she was grateful for the time she did get to spend with Him. She was not prepared for what was to come in the months ahead. She never knew her newfound friend meant so much to her.

~ * ~

He had been gone for only a few months but Angelina missed going to the cave to talk with Him. She often thought about those moments and the time they had spent together. It was only a brief time but she was aware of the amazing impact that God had left on her life. Then she remembered that He said that she could talk to the Holy Spirit. He said they were the same. With an excitement she almost couldn't contain she jumped up and spread her wings to dive off the mountainside. It had been a few months but her wings couldn't get her there fast enough. She was cutting through the air and her wings were blades slicing through the wind like a knife through butter. She reached the waterfall and she was surprised that the mouth of the cave was so overgrown with waterfall greenery and vines. Since she and the Lord were no longer meeting there apparently no one else used the cave either. Unsure of what awaited her inside, she landed quietly and pushed her snout into the vines to enter the cave. It was dark and she had to give her eyes a minute to adjust to her surroundings. Once they were acclimated, she softly walked past the water. Her scales were on high alert and ready to disappear to the spirit realm as soon as any danger presented itself. However, so far so good.

The sound of the water cascading off the cliff above was the only sound she could hear. Disappointed in their absence she coiled up and laid down on the cool rock floor. She couldn't understand where she went wrong. Did she misunderstand Him? He said that the Holy Spirit was always with her and He would never leave her. All she had to do was call on His name. Then it hit her. She had not called on Him. "Lord? Are you there?" She waited patiently. "You said that the Holy Spirit and you were the same and that you would never leave me." The waterfalls seemed to get louder as the silence was overwhelming her heart. She knew that it was too good to be true. No one in her life has ever stayed with her. They have always left her and she has always had to fend for herself. How could she let her heart believe Him? Her fear and doubt continued to close her heart back to the stone it was originally before God came into her life. She lay there still and quiet. Her mind concentrated on how wonderful it was to open her heart and feel joy again.

However, here she was again. Leaning out the mouth of the cave, she laid her head down on the rocks away from the falling water. Overlooking the forest below. All alone and no one to care if she was dead or alive. That was one thing she wished had never changed. She felt like someone cared for her. Someone was interested in her ideas, thoughts, and plans for her day. She never realized that when He was here. That He cared and that she liked that about them. At least with her family, she was born invisible. They never asked her about her day or what her plans were. They never doted or loved on her. The only time she felt like she made a difference to them was when she got lost and they were inconvenienced to look for her. But when God was in her life, He asked her how her day was and He cared whether it was good or bad. She never knew she was lonely until after He was gone. She had so much to tell Him about the months they were separated. Now she just held her head with such despair. She didn't want to be alone again.

"Angelina, why would you be alone again?" He asked. Still laying down with her head buried in her arms and her tears pouring down the rocks to the waterfalls below. Through her sobs, she answered Him. "I am alone because you are not here like you said you would be." She breathes in and out then settles back into her sadness. "I didn't realize that I never wanted to be alone again. I was thrilled to remember that you said that you were leaving the Holy Spirit to be with me to guide me as I went forward, but He is not here. You are not here and then He is not here. My family and my friends are not here. I have no one." She continued to cry through her despair. She fell asleep not realizing He was there talking to her.

~ * ~

She woke up feeling a little hazy-eyed. Remembering the night before, she sat up. Still in the cave. Still alone like the night before. She scratched her head because she could swear that she recalled a conversation she had when she thought she was alone. However, her memories were recalling that she was not alone. He was talking with her. God was there. She was so saddened that He was not there that she didn't even realize that she was mistaken. She went to sleep talking to God. She shook her head, feeling ridiculous now. He must think I'm an idiot…

"God? Are you still here?" she asked. Not expecting Him to have stayed just for her.

"Yes, I am here. I never left." He replied to her question.

"I can't believe that you came. I also cannot believe that you stayed all night just for me." She said unsure of why he cared for her so much. She felt like she was a burden to worry about. Her family always made her feel like she was such a pain to take care of. Like her breathing was costing them gold they did not have to spend on her. Here she was sitting in a cave with the Lord of the Universe and He constantly tells her she is loved, wanted, and needed by Him. But she had nothing ever to offer Him. She didn't have any riches or any mountain of gold she could give Him. No animals, plants, or harvest from land that she could offer Him as a sacrifice. No castle full of her servants for him to use. All she had was herself. Her loyalty, faithfulness, and her love. Her heart that her family had stomped all over. She admitted that her heart was broken and shattered into a million pieces by others who were supposed to love her but only proved in the end that they did not care. Not really. But she offered her heart anyways. It was not much but it was all that she had to give Him.

He humbly accepted it with great care and told her that He would take great care of all the broken pieces she was giving Him. He said that when He was done repairing her heart it would be stronger than it had ever been before. He told her that He would give her heart back to her, healed. Healed and ready to love again. His words felt real but she knew how small the pieces of her heart were broken into. There was no way anyone, no matter how good they were, could ever fix her heart. She knew that He was one day going to hand it back to her and he would have to tell her He was sorry. That it wasn't able to be fixed. She just knew that was what was going to happen. She would bet her life on it. She sat resolved that she was right and that He didn't know what He was getting Himself into. It was okay. He was there and He was her friend. Nothing could cloud her happy day.

They spent the whole day together. She had never spent the day talking and reminiscing over past events with anyone like she had today. The only thing she could ever ask any more of God was for Him to be a real dragon so that she could see His face and touch His arm when they walked. He told her that He would bring to her a dragon that He had made specific to who she needed him to be. He would have given his heart to God to heal too. Only then would he be worthy of her love. Because until they give their heart to God to heal all the broken pieces they could never love another the way they needed to be loved. If they did they would only be loving with a broken, ugly heart. The love would be distorted and would have bad growth coming off of it. It would be jagged and sharp. It would only be able to love in a way that was meant to hurt others. It could never be the best heart it wanted to be without God. Angelina thought she understood what He was talking about but she still wasn't sure of it all.

She longed to have a family one day. She wanted a really big family. With lots of kids running around. She has imagined herself being a really good mom. She always hated thinking this way, but a better mother to her kids than her mother was to her. She would never make her daughter feel like she was a burden to love and care for. When she thought about having a daughter she always thought about the fun things they would do together. All the wonderful things she would teach her about being a female dragon. She would raise her to be a great mother. She would be able to handle anything her family would throw her way. She would be the best. She looked forward to this day. She has dreamed about this day ever since she was little and could start imagining what a different family would be like. A loving, caring family that didn't always want to hunt, kill, and destroy the world. She could never understand why her family was like that. Always looking for destruction. It was as if someone came in with all the worst ways to hurt others and taught them how to be mean dragons. All she ever sought after was to do good to others.

She could never imagine being like her mother who yelled and screamed ugly, hurtful things to her babies. She never liked it when her mother did those things to her and her brothers. I mean she understood that her brothers frustrated their daily limits out of their mother but to tell them that she wished they had never been born. What was the need for them to ever hear that? Their mother often confused Angelina. She could never understand her. It was as if they were from two different worlds. She had concluded a long time ago that the only reason for a mother to be and act that horrible was to breed hatred, destruction, and evil in them. One day her mother said something to her brother that was truly profound. She told them that if she didn't teach them to be hard and powerful then the world would rip them up and throw them away. They had to learn to not be so sensitive and to take everything the world had to give because the people in this world wouldn't go to help or give them anything. They had to rely on themselves. Which she thought was funny because Angelina thought that way about her family. None of them gave her food, love, or help. She had to care for herself; all alone and it was hard for her.

She couldn't wait for the day when she would find another male dragon and they would have a great little family together. She wondered what he would be like. What he would look like? Would his scales be the same color and shape as hers? Would he be really tall? Or short and close to the ground? Would his horns be curved or straight? She saw a male dragon one time and he had straight horns. They followed the sides of his face and head then went up and turned into each other at the end. Her horns were big and they curved in one big twirl and they ended behind her ears at the top of her head. They were strong and solid white. Her scales were dark shades of gray and black with hues of red in the bright sunlight. Her claws were soft and padded. She loved her feet. When she walked she never made a sound. It was because she kept her nails so short. Her mother hated it when they woke her up from sleep. So Angelina thought it was best if she eliminated any chance of that happening on her part. It was hard enough keeping her long tail from hitting and making dragging noises through the forest floor.

She had a really long tail and at the end of the scales, two fins shaped an ace at the end. She loved her tail during a hunt because she could use her tail as a weapon. In many different fashions. It was long and could be swung like a tree to hit something or knock them down from the air. Then if needed the end was perfect for smacking something really hard. She slapped a deer one time and knocked him out with one swing. It was then she realized how useful her tail was to her. That was when she wondered what else she could do.

~ * ~

Angelina already knew she could disappear and escape into the spirit realm to get away from danger. That was where she discovered God and where they became such good friends. She loved having the ability to get away quickly. It became very useful in dangerous situations but she wondered how else she could use it. Did she have to disappear from this realm totally or could she become unseen but still be here? When she first started camouflaging from danger she thought she was only disappearing their sight. Blending into her background. Not actually leaving the area completely. So after she realized her tail was a good hunting tool and her paws were quiet when walking, she decided she needed to explore what else she could do.

As she walked with God, He was telling her about when He was creating all the animals that would live on Earth. He told her about some amazing creatures that swam in the big waters that He called an ocean. They were warm-blooded like her but they could swim in the deep depths of the water for a very long time but then they would eventually have to come back up to the top of the water to take a deep breath. He told her about this animal that lived in the desert plains that was spotted and could run faster than any other cat. He called them a Cheetah. He talked about some of His creations that could do several incredible things. She longed to see these animals one day. She was amazed by their characteristics and abilities to do great things she could never imagine. He spoke of this one animal that lived in the rivers and they would create their homes out of big trees. They would chop the trees down with their teeth by gnawing at the wood into little pieces. Then they would lay the branches and limbs of the tree in the water across the two sides and it would stop the water from flowing down the river. When they did that they were creating a little pool for their young to swim in and would catch the fish in the pool to eat.

Each animal He created had a great purpose and a way of doing things. They each had a different way to care for their young. They ate different foods. Some ate other animals after they killed them and some only ate plants or vegetation. Some ate bugs and flies while others ate trees and their fruits. But one thing she realized when He was talking was that He was proud of each one. He loved everything about them. They were His creation. Each was unique and different from other animals. However, He loved them all the same. Regardless of her opinions of their differences, He called them all good. He talked to her about their purposes and why He created them that way. She listened and replied when she had a question or two but she couldn't interrupt His excitement. Their walk led them back to the cave. This is where He began to tell her about the dragon and the reason why He created them.

It was then that she sat down and realized her life did have a purpose. It was then she found out that she was not created for destruction or killing. She was created to lead and to serve humans. She was created to love them and to help them in their journey. That was why she felt so different from other dragons. She was not created for this life. Unfortunately, that answer only led her to more questions. If dragons weren't created to live this way then why were they like this? She went to sleep wondering about these questions. She made a point to remember to ask God about this tomorrow. She always looked forward to tomorrow. She liked having someone to care about her and to wonder how she was. She had never had a father in her life. Remember, he left their family before she was born. So she never knew what it felt like to have one in her life. But since God has come into her life it has felt like He was her father. At least that's how she felt a father should be to her. Guiding her and giving her His wisdom when she needed it. Telling her stories about His past and the things He has gone through. Sharing His feelings and thoughts with her to help her understand the way that the world works.

Now that she understands who He had created her to be, it was her mission to be the best dragon she could be to honor Him and His Legacy in her. Instead of hurting and killing humans, she was going to help them and guide them back to God and teach them about His Love for them. After hearing God's Heart for them they surely would want to worship and be with Him again too. Now she just had to figure out how to get them to listen to her and trust her. She was a large dragon after all and dragons have been known to kill a few humans in their life. She had so much she had to overcome to do what she was created for. She not only had to help them overcome their fear of her and to have an open heart to listen to what she had to say. She also had to convince them that they were wrong about God.

Chapter Six: Evil Crouching

6

Alexander flew all night. He pushed through his hunger, pain, and fear to reach the land where he heard the castle of the breeder was. It felt like he had been flying forever when he began to see a small flickering of lights along the coastline of a small town on the land. Which was perfect timing because he was overdue for a break. His muscles were burning and his thirst was unbearable. The mist of saltwater floating in the air became heavy over time. The sailors he overheard talking about the breeder said that one would know he was at the right place on the coastline because after you saw the little town of lights you would see a big rotating light shining over the sea to warn the ships of the coast. He said right above the rotating light was a bunch of lights on the mountain above the town and that was the breeder's castle. Alexander saw exactly what he was talking about. It could not have been described any better for Alexander.

Alexander was thankful the castle was on the mountainside because that was perfect coverage for a dragon to be in. Alexander knew he was going to need rest and water as soon as he landed. He wished he had thought this part of the trip through a little better. He would have figured out where he was going to land to rest and figure out his next steps. Well, there was nothing that could be done about it now. He began to get closer to the lights and he knew that he had to rise above the clouds to be able to look over the mountains for a cave and for fresh water for him to drink. As he rose he spotted a big light shining through the darkness through the sky. This light was not stationary and it was pointing into the clouds in the sky like it was searching for something flying. Alexander responded quickly and rose high into the upper cloud coverage. It was a good thing that he responded so quickly because they would've spotted him and that could be disastrous for Alexander's plans to rescue his parents.

He rose high so that he could not be seen but he couldn't rise too high for he was supposed to be looking for a safe place to land to get out of the skies before the sunlight took away his ability to hide. It didn't take him long. He flew further north away from the castle and from any signs of humans. He found water and a large cave high in the mountains. He landed just in time for the sun was coming up on the horizon and declare its existence to that side of the world. It was cold in the cave. The top was covered in ice and snow. Deep inside the cave ran a small stream of water through the caves. Alexander wasn't sure he wouldn't drink it dry soon. He was parched. After he drank all he could he crawled deeper into the cave and started a fire to warm the rock for him to rest. He had to make sure that he was deep inside the cave so that the fire's light could not be seen by people. Alexander rested for several hours until his stomach told him it was time for him to get up and eat. He tried to ignore his stomach and its growing attempts to get his attention. After a while, he could no longer bear the burden. It had been a long night and he had to restore the energy that he spent flying there.

That's when he decided to venture away from the cave for a little bit to scope out the area for food. He was fortunate because the mouth of the cave pointed away from people's civilizations and he was deep enough into the forest that he would never be seen by people. These mountains were not habitable to people. They had tall and sharp ridges and there were not many flat areas to put a house or building. So it was a perfect sanctuary for a dragon to be at. Places this high up usually were a perfect hunting ground for a dragon because they could kill large animals like bears and elk without being seen too easily. It did not take him long to find his meal but as he was swooping down to kill the bear by the stream of water coming down the mountain he saw a couple of men looking at the bear as well. Alexander flew up into the trees in the mountains and clung to the tops of the pines masking his shape from the hunters below him. He was surprised they could stand the cold this far up into the mountains.

He noticed they wore different clothes. Furs around their heads and they were covered almost entirely by clothing. He guessed to help keep them warm. They looked strange to him compared to the humans where he came from. These humans carried long metal-handled rods they threw over their shoulders. He wasn't sure what they were for until they used them to kill the bear. A loud bang sounded and something flew out the end of it and hit the bear in the head. The bear died instantly and they walked to claim their prize from the forest. They began to cut its fur off its body and into smaller portions that were easier for them to carry. Alexander had never seen that before and he was alarmed. Alarmed and intrigued all at the same time. His curiosity overcame his need for food. He wanted to know more about these people. He quietly followed them to see where they were going. They led him to a small house in the next valley over away from the stream. The house was covered in snow and you could tell it was warm. There was a pillar of smoke that rose from the top that smelled of many different things Alexander could not figure out. They smelled good. He wanted to know what they were. The smells made him remember that he was famished. But he couldn't go away yet. He wanted to know more about them.

Alexander stayed in the shadows of the trees until after the sun went down. He had watched the family of four all day long. He watched them do all sorts of different things. He found himself several times almost speaking to them about a better way to do what they were doing but he caught himself before he did. He couldn't figure out why he was so intrigued by them. The older man had a soft strength about him. His words were always few but he never had to repeat himself when he spoke. When he spoke to his sons he radiated fatherly wisdom and his guidance spoke truth you could trust in. Alexander had never seen a father like him. Alexander wanted to talk to him and learn from him. It felt like he had so much to glean from his years. He wanted to help him with the farm chores and help him dig that bunch of tree roots up in the back of the house that Alexander could see he had been working on for a while now.

The mother was just as strong and as soft as the father was. There was peace in their home that Alexander had never felt before. The property felt free the closer Alexander got to it. She never had to scream and yell at her kids like other women did. Her children were good listeners and they were well-behaved. Alexander felt like this family had stepped out of another world. They were not like other families that he had observed before. There was a glow around them. The glow never created a shadow or a mark on the space or things around the people or the ground. The light that surrounded their home and around their barn. It was emanating from within. Yet there was no visible source. A fire creates light and can be touched. It can be seen coming from the burning wood but this light was just there. As Alexander watched from afar for several days, there were predator animals that would come down the valley hills towards their home and the barn full of horses and pigs. Alexander was invested in their well-being without even realizing he cared. His spine full of angular scales stood at attention and ready to step in and attack the animals before they could enter the property but Alexander never had to engage them. The animals always veered away from the house as soon as they came close to the glow around the property. It was as if this light that covered them was protecting them from harm. Alexander couldn't understand it.

His curiosity brought him to a place where he needed to see what it was. It was late in the afternoon on a gloomy rainy day but this light was still present. Alexander felt it was a perfect day for him to come down out of the shadows of the trees and feel this light for himself. He wanted to see what it would do if Alexander got closer to the house. The family was inside for most of the day because of the hard rain that was coming down. So Alexander felt it was the perfect time for him to see more about this light. As he climbed down from the branches and down onto the pine needles on the forest floor, the water ran down his body softly. The wet ground padded his movements. The evening sun got darker and provided Alexander with the safety to move closer to the house. He could see the glow and as Alexander moved closer he started to get anxious. Almost afraid that the light would hurt him once he stepped into the property. Would it radiate electricity that would sting him to keep him away from the house? He stepped just beyond the light and looked at the home from behind the barn. He looked at the ground, preparing to step closer to the barn. His paws stepped over the line of glowing light onto the father's ground. A warmth could be felt throughout his body. As he stepped over he closed his eyes because from the moment his snout crossed the line the warmth radiated through him. He felt the peace come over his soul and the raging war of his past melted away into the vast space of the mountains into the darkness. Alexander was overcome with emotion, so he lay down on the ground behind the barn and allowed the tears to fall from his eyes.

"Hello, Alexander. I have been waiting a while for you to come."

Alexander alarmed sprung up from laying down position to sitting up. Looking around to see who was talking to him. He was surprised to see that it was the father that he thought was inside with his family.

"Don't be afraid. I am not here to hurt you. I was told you would one day come and would need help. I have been prepared for your visit." The man said to him.

Alexander wasn't sure what was going on here. Should he leave and get to safety? The man began to slowly move around him and he walked into the large barn door to go inside away from the rain. There was something about the man that Alexander wasn't afraid of him. He didn't feel like he was there to hurt Alexander. However, he needed to keep at a distance to be sure. So he just followed the man with his eyes.

"Alexander, God told me many years ago that you would come to me and that you would crave to know more about the goodness of people. God told me that you would not hurt me and that you wanted to get to know me better. Is that true?" he asked.

Alexander still cautious, shook his head up and down signifying confirmation to his question. He couldn't believe this man was standing before him asking him these things. Where were his sons? Were they around him somewhere planning to trap him and kill him? Alexander frantically looked around trying to spot the young men.

"You don't need to worry, The rest of the family is inside with their mother staying safe. We weren't sure that you wouldn't cause us harm. So we kept the little ones inside away from you, just in case something went wrong." The man said realizing that Alexander was alarmed and worried about other humans. Alexander calmed down just a little but still worried about what could happen. He could feel his spine scales were still alert. Alexander had never talked to a human before. Does he speak dragon? Alexander thought for a moment and concluded that he could understand the language the man spoke. Maybe this God of his was helping them understand one another. He decided to speak to this man.

"How do you know my name?" Alexander asked him.

The man stopped pacing turned his head and looked at Alexander. He had a surprised look on his face. Almost like he wasn't sure he was going to understand a dragon talking to him. He gathered himself and then continued to pace around the barn as he spoke.

"As I said, God told me many years ago that you would come to me wanting to know more about humans. I was praying to God that He would give direction to me and my wife's life and He spoke to me. He told me to keep seeking God and following His path for me. He said that one day a dragon would come to me and his name would be Alexander. God said that you wouldn't be a threat to me and that I was to teach you about Him and I was to be your friend. We have been waiting for a long time for you to come. I am so happy to meet you." The man told Alexander.

"Can I ask you what your name is?" Alexander asked.

"You can call me Baldwin. My name means friend."

"Thank you, Baldwin," Alexander said.

"For what?"

"For being my friend."

"Well, in this case, you can thank God, because it was God who prepared your way" Baldwin replied.

~ * ~

After that day Alexander and Baldwin became great friends. Alexander was up every day early in the morning. Anxious to start learning all he could from him. Baldwin was guided by God to teach Alexander all he needed to know about the relationship between God and humans. In exchange, Alexander was willing to be there to help him and his family do anything they needed him to do. Alexander was a great helper. The more he learned who they were the easier it was to anticipate what they needed from him. Months went by and he had forgotten why he came to this place to begin with. In the mountain valley with Baldwin and his family, they lived peacefully with no troubles. Alexander was a part of their family and he cared for them like they were his. Which reminded Alexander why he was there at all. He was reminded of the mother and father he had lost when he was a young dragon. He was torn on who he wanted to become. On one hand, he could seek out what happened to his family, or on the other, he could stay and live in peace with Baldwin and his family.

He struggled with this for many months until one day Baldwin confronted him about what was bothering him. Alexander told Baldwin everything. He shared with him all that led him to be there and the dilemma that he now faced. Baldwin stopped for a moment and thought to himself. He sat down on the wooden tree stump by the barn and lit his cherry cigar before he answered. Crossing his left leg over his right before he carefully spoke. It was as if he was waiting for his reply to come to him. Baldwin did this a lot. He sat patiently before he could figure out what he was supposed to say to Alexander. Like he was waiting for the particulars to be delivered to his mouth from another part of his body. However, when the reply finally did come out of Baldwin's mouth it was remarkably worth the wait.

"Alexander, God says that our will is our own. He says that you may choose to follow your mind or your heart down a path but neither will be without pain and heartache. God says that He will be with you no matter which road you choose to walk on." Baldwin said as the sweet smoke surrounded them and filled the hazy, rainy valley. He told Alexander about the Son of God who came to live on Earth as a human. He lived and taught the people about how to live the way God wanted them to live. To only live doing good and to follow the Light. That God's way was the only way that you could go to Heaven and be with God for eternity. He told him that the only way you could become like God's Son was to accept His Son, Christ as your Lord and Savior. To say that He died on the cross to save us from punishment for the sins that we had committed against God. That through His Son Christ Jesus we were saved. Baldwin helped Alexander pray a prayer that accepted God as his too. Alexander said the prayer and felt at peace within his heart. But he was still unsure what he needed to do about the difficult choice that he needed to make.

Normally Baldwin's words of wisdom helped Alexander come to a conclusion easily but today he felt more confused with his response. Alexander always thought there was a right way and a wrong way to do everything. The right way always led to good things and the wrong way always led to death and destruction. His choices up to now have always been clear to decide and Alexander always chose to follow the righteous path. But he didn't feel good about either of the paths that lay before him, He nodded his head to Baldwin who got up from the stump and walked inside the house. Alexander coiled up inside the barn and stared up the mountainside.

~ * ~

He had fallen asleep listening to the wind lightly rustling the trees. But he woke to the sound of metal armor clinking and men yelling. Alarmed he peeked through two loose boards in the barn wall facing the front of the house. He could see a bunch of men running down the road toward the house. Baldwin came out of the front of his home with a cigar in his mouth asking them what they wanted and why they were there. Alexander could sense that Baldwin was upset. He didn't like those men being at his house. Two of the men grabbed Baldwin and started to drag him back to the house. Alexander took a big deep breath and was getting ready to fly up out from behind the barn to attack these men hurting Baldwin. Baldwin began to scream out loud, "Get out of here! You're in danger! Leave and get somewhere safe! Now!"

Alexander knew he was talking to him but Alexander couldn't leave them in danger like this. He swore in his heart that he was going to help them and protect them when Baldwin and he became friends. He couldn't leave them now! He quietly shook his head and snuffed at Baldwin's instructions. One of the men who was leading this attack started to scream out in the valley loudly.

"We don't want the people. We are here for you! Come out and let us take you in and we won't hurt the people. If you don't come out we will kill this man and we will set the home on fire with the woman and the kids trapped inside! Is that what you want? You only have a few moments to think it over. My master wants you for himself and has permitted us to do whatever is necessary to bring you back to the castle." The man said holding a burning stick up in the air as he yelled.

Baldwin screamed out, "That's not true! You need to leave!"

The other man escorting Baldwin kicked his legs out from under him and pushed his neck down into the ground to keep Baldwin from speaking anymore. Baldwin fell to his knees and he laid his head down on his forearms laying on the ground. Alexander flew up into the night sky; spreading his wings out in full. Coming out from behind the barn where he was hiding. He wanted to face this threat. He wanted to be closer to Baldwin and the men who were attacking him. That would be the last hand that man would lay on his friend. Alexander was sure of that.

"That will be the last time you strike my friend. I promise you that." Alexander said. His eyebrows were firm and his eyes were flint. He was ready to attack. He was ready to save his friend and his family. The man who held Baldwin down to the ground as his prisoner jumped at the threat made by Alexander and put a knife to Baldwin's throat. He smiled as he looked over to the man making all the demands. Alarmed Alexander froze; worried for Baldwin.

"If I let you take me to your master, then you will leave the people alone?"

"Yes, that's what I said. Did I not?" said the man.

"You did, but how do I know you're not lying to me?" Alexander questioned.

Alexander was frozen with fear. His eyes may not have shown it but his heart would have if you could see it. Baldwin had always talked about this God that saved him in the past. God led him from a life of pain, anger, and murder. God would speak to him and lead him away from doing bad things. Baldwin told him of several times in his past when Baldwin had a choice to do evil or to do good and God would speak to his spirit and his mind. He would convince him to go towards the light. To do good instead of darkness. Baldwin spoke of this God as if He were real and alive. That in his times of distress or worry all Baldwin said he needed to do was call out His name. Or he could whisper His name and He was there. He would answer and help Baldwin. Baldwin gave credit for bringing him his wife, Annabeth. Alexander felt so unsure of believing in someone who could help but was not there in body only in spirit. What good was helping with just His Words? Alexander always thought that if he truly needed help he wouldn't be calling on someone to talk him through his dilemma. He would be calling on someone to help him get free or out of his bondages. Alexander was afraid. He couldn't think of a better time to call on this God for help.

In his mind, he called out God's name. "God, if you're real. If you're there. Would you come to me now?"

He waited for an answer. The moment felt as if it took forever. As if time slowed down just for this moment for Alexander to meet his creator. For Him to speak and for Alexander to hear His Truth for himself. The threat around Baldwin and himself grew with every second that passed by.

"Yes, Alexander. I am here." A voice in his heart said. He didn't know where the voice came from and he did not hear it with his ears. But he knew he heard it. He knew God was there with him. Baldwin was speaking the truth. Someone spoke to him and His Voice was Truth. It was real. He was there with Alexander. He felt His Presence comforting him in this moment of despair and fear.

"God, Baldwin told me about the times that you saved him in his past. He needs your help now. He is in grave danger and I don't want him or his family to get hurt. Can you make him and his family disappear to safety?" Alexander pleaded with God. "Can you save him?"

"I wish that I could, but if I stepped in Alexander, what would be the point of free will?"

"He won't have free will any longer, God. He'll be dead. These men will kill them." Alexander cried out in his heart.

"I'm sorry, Alexander. I told you both paths were not without pain and heartache. I am with you. You are stronger than you think you are. Remember why you were created. Remember your promise."

Well, He was no help. What do I do now? Remember why I was created?!? What a load of rubbish! If He could step in and save Baldwin and He loves Baldwin, then why wouldn't He save them? What is the point of being an all-mighty God if you don't use your power for anything? What was the point of me calling on a God who won't do anything to help me? Free will?!? WHAT IS THE POINT OF FREE WILL?!? If men use their free will to hurt others and kill? If their free will is to do the will of the darkness then where are those who will fight to do only the good in this world? Where are the ones who use the Light to dispel the deeds of darkness? Remember why I was created? He never told me what I was created for. No one has ever told me what I was created for. Alexander's thoughts were only frustrating the matter and making it worse. Next thing he knows Baldwin is screaming at him…

"It's okay! We believe in Him. We will go to Heaven! You can't save us all, Alexander!"

Baldwin shoves the man holding him captive runs away from the men with the guns and runs towards his wife and boys.

Alexander recollects God's Words to him, "Remember your promise!" He remembers the promise he made to himself when Baldwin and He became friends. He promised to help them and to protect them. That was it!! He knew what he had to do. He was the Light. He flew between the men and Baldwin with his family; he opened his wings, took a big deep breath, and laid a blanket of fire across everything that threatened them. The army of men with their guns opened fire on Alexander. Guns were going off all around them and smoke filled the air in the little homestead valley. A wall of fire protected Baldwin and his family. They were behind Alexander, curled up on the ground; terrified of the bullets and fire destroying everything they owned. The bullets whizzed by them and pierced wood, the barn, and the house's windows. The fire killing everyone standing on the wrong side of the war.

Alexander had done it. He understood what God meant about free will. It was up to those who believed in Him to do the will of the Light to dispel the darkness of the world. It was up to the Light Bearers to help others to grow, heal, and aid those who needed help in their times of distress. God was doing something when He was called on. He was strengthening His Light Bearers to make a difference. God was there. He felt Him with him as Alexander slumped over against the mountainside. Alexander knew what he was created for. He was created to protect his friends. He was created to save Baldwin, Annabeth, and the boys. He closed his eyes. He was tired. He just wanted to rest for a little while. The thing he saw was Baldwin and his family running to his side. Baldwin and Annabeth crying as they ran to him.

In Alexander's last breath, he illuminated a glow that burned from the inside of his heart. He was a Light Bearer just like his father always told him he'd be. He was chosen to serve God in Heaven with the League of Protectors. He now is serving God with the greatest honors. His Light still protects men from the darkness.

~ * ~

Ziggy stayed quiet and hid in the darkness of the forest path for as long as he could stand it. Aaron didn't know what to do. His father was always the one who took care of him and protected him in the forest. Aaron just lay there crying on his father's chest. He didn't know what else to do. He didn't know the way home from here. Ziggy sat there and contemplated what he should do. If he revealed his presence there with Aaron it could frighten him more and put Ziggy in danger if the father woke up and was aware of him. They could come back after they get help and hunt Ziggy down to kill him. Ziggy didn't want that to happen. On the other hand, Aaron was alone and the man needed help. If the trap had cut something important in the man's leg he could die quickly. Ziggy didn't want that either.

Ziggy decided that he was going to reveal himself and be the one in danger. If he could convince Aaron that his father needed to be helped then maybe they would forgive him for being there. Ziggy spoke out loud to Aaron from behind the trees and brush. Hoping to give Aaron the chance to be ready for him to show himself eventually.

"Are you okay, young man?" Ziggy said.

Aaron alarmed at the voice, sat up and asked, "Who said that? Come out and show yourself!"

"I will come out from behind the tree but you have to promise me that you won't be afraid and scream. Can you do that? I want to help you and your father."

"I can do that," Aaron said calmly; unsure of what he was about to see. Was it a man who was disfigured? Was it a ghost or a monster? Should he be worried? Aaron stood up from his father still lying on the ground. Aaron picked up a stick just in case he needed to fight something off and protect his father.

Ziggy walked out from behind the trees and into the small stream of sunlight coming in from above. His blue scales glittered in the light. Ziggy made sure to lower his head to Aaron when he got closer to him. Hoping to show him that he wasn't a threat to him. Lowing his head and eyes signifying submission to his authority. Aaron's eyes got as big as the unripe green walnuts hanging on the trees. He didn't know what to call this thing. "What are you?" Aaron said holding his stick up in the air.

"My name is Ziggy. I am a dragon. I will not harm you or your father. Can I come closer to him and look to see if I can help him get freed from the trap?" Ziggy offered.

Aaron looked down at his father, shook his head yes, and then stepped to the side to allow Ziggy through to him. Ziggy assessed Aaron's father and concluded that he was not in any immediate danger. Ziggy pulled apart the claws of the trap that had enclosed around his ankle to free him of it. He then asked Aaron if they had any shirts or wrapping to cover the cut on his leg till they got somewhere safer and with more supplies than the forest floor. Aaron looked in his father's bag, found a clean shirt, and handed it to Ziggy. Ziggy and Aaron wrapped the leg as best they could.

"Aaron, can you help me get you and your father on my back so that I can take you to your home?" Aaron agreed and began to lift his father under his father's arms to set him up. Ziggy used his snout to carry the man up onto his back until Aaron could climb up and gather his father onto his back between Ziggy's shoulders Ziggy carefully flew through the forest close to the floor just in case they got unsettled on Ziggy's back. Nothing would be worse than having them fall off during their rescue.

Once they reached their home, Aaron called and ran into the house for his mother and older brother. They ran out of the house and suddenly stopped alarmed by Ziggy's presence. He lowered his snout and eyes to show them he was not a threat to them. Aaron explained what had happened in the woods and how Ziggy saved them. Aaron's brother ran up to Ziggy's side and helped Aaron get their father down. Aaron's mother had run back into the house to get some supplies to tend to his wounds. They carried him into the house and left Ziggy outside by himself. Ziggy felt all alone and unsure that he had done the right thing. Should he fly away and get somewhere safe? Or should he stay and wait to see if the man was okay? Right about the time Ziggy had decided to leave and had turned away from the house and opened his wings, Aaron came running out the screened-in porch door and flung his arms around Ziggy's neck.

"Thank you, Ziggy. You saved my life and my father's life. Thank you."

He left Ziggy to run back inside with his family. The older brother stood on the porch waving his hand goodbye and nodded his head in thankfulness before they went back inside the home. Ziggy was relieved with his decision. Despite the dangers that he faced he had helped those humans to get to safety and had done his best to heal the man. He knew now in his heart that he had done the right thing and that he was proud of the work he had done. Ziggy smiled and looked up into the sky. He then felt a warmth come over his body.

"You have done a great thing here, Ziggy. I am proud of you." The warmth that came over him began to glow; radiating from inside his heart. At that moment, he was honored and disappeared and went to Heaven to serve God on the League of Protectors. He had become who God had created him to be.

~ * ~

Thankfully Angelina's induction into the League of Protectors wasn't as painful as Alexander's. She didn't have to die to be honored. Nor was it as dangerous as Ziggy's. Angelina became a great leader to the humans fleeing from a great war nearby. She gathered and led groups of people to safety away from the shooting and fighting. She kept them safe despite all they were facing and provided them with safe passage through great mountain regions to a safer place to live. Hiding them and feeding them as they fled from the war. She never had to hurt anyone in her path to righteousness. She just had to be confident in who God had created her to be and walk it out with the humans. She brought many people to safety.

Her continued relationship with God in the Spirit realm gave her a great assurance that God was always with her and teaching her new things. He was her constant guide in the rough mountainside to guide many humans who were fleeing to a safer life. She was also able to tell many of them about God and how great He was to her. Her testimony was told and retold all through the generations of humans who became believers in God. Every group of people she came into contact with she shared the truth of who God was and how they were loved. For many years, she gave them hope and peace as they traveled many miles to safety. She lived a long and faithful life serving God here on Earth. However, her body was not as capable as it once was. She walked slower these days and she became out of breath faster. But her duty was to do as the Lord needed her to, so she did. Everyday. Angelina went to sleep in her cave one day after a long trip. There was no great cloud of witnesses or parades when she was honored. She closed her eyes and told God goodnight.

He answered her, "Goodnight good and faithful servant." Her body became warm and she glowed so radiantly that the Light filled the dark cave like the sun. She disappeared from the cave and was honored by God. She woke up in Heaven with a new, younger body. She was free like a new baby dragon who had learned how to fly for the first time. She was clear of mind and her tail was again as sharp as a sword. Her tail whipped as it once did through the tree branches. She was honored for her faithfulness and was asked to serve God once more in the League of Protectors.

~ * ~

No one knows when darkness has begun its descent upon their life. One doesn't wake up to a beautiful morning with the songbirds singing and the sun shining. Then decide to be used for evil. It always comes in when you least expect it. Evil comes in and tells you the simplest of lies to make the worst version of yourself you can be. If you're not paying close attention you won't even know it's happening to you. You will eventually believe it was your idea. You believe that you're doing what you're supposed to do. Then one day you wake up covered in something awful and you're shaking you're head wondering how your life got to be this bad.

The Fallen Ones didn't just gather in the forest one day and decided that they wanted to throw God out of Heaven. They didn't plot against the good that was in the universe and decided to war against it. Each dragon had overcome their own set of evils in their childhood to get them to adulthood. Then once they reached righteousness and fulfilled their purpose they were then chosen for the League of

Protectors to join God in Heaven. They all had a close, intimate relationship with God when they were chosen to serve Him. They all loved God for all He had done for them. They each had their testimony of who God was to them. They were not blind to the greatness of God's Love. So needless to say but I will say it anyway and make it clear to you now. The darkness in the world does not care who you are. It will do whatever it can to kill, steal, and destroy the goodness in you. It will manipulate you to make you fall from the Light and it will drag you through the mud. The darkness wants to destroy everything in its path and it will stop at nothing until it has pulled you from glory into the shadows writhing in sadness.

Drake was once a respected and honorable dragon. But you wouldn't recognize him as a good dragon by who he is today. The darkness crept in on Drake when he thought he was safe. Drake was God's first dragon honored to become a protector in Heaven. When God created the dragons He created many different types, styles, gifts, and personalities. In the beginning, only twelve dragons were created to serve the Lord in Heaven. Those first twelve were wonderous creatures. They guided and helped humans keep the peace while they worshiped God in Heaven. They were so patient and kind. There was a dragon for every need you might have. But as they began to have families and grow larger in numbers God wanted to share them with humans before they reached Heaven. So they were sent to Earth to begin their life there. Over time both humans and dragons gave in to the darkness. Hurting each other and themselves.

Darkness comes in and slowly changes how you think about things. It tells you that there's an ugly truth in what the darkness wants you to see. That somehow the good in the world isn't really what it seems. It takes the very foundation of your truths and confuses them just a little. God says not to lie and we aren't lying. We're just not telling them the whole truth. We justify the reasoning for everything we want to do. God tells us to honor our Father and our Mother but yet we talk bad about them behind their backs. We judge the way they raised us as if we know better than they do. Honor is not a reflection of whether or not they deserve it. Honoring someone says more about who you are as an individual. My father may have not been the best father to me in my opinion but how I honor him says I saw the mistakes, I learned from his errors, and I stand here loving him anyway. Giving thanks to him because he taught me to be better than he is. God wants us to listen and hear these truths about life, not to restrict or confine our way of life but to give us a more fruitful and abundant life. Full of joy and peace. However, not everyone hears God and gets to know who He is as God, our Father. We make up our minds about who we think He should be and condemn Him if He is not what we want Him to be.

That's where Drake and the Fallen Ones were manipulated out of grace and wisdom. The darkness tricks you and makes you think, see, and hear things that aren't the truth. It lies to you to get you to see what it wants you to see. It manipulates the truth to distort your reality. It makes you think that you have uncovered some secret to the universe and revealed some hidden secret that God didn't want you to know and that it's up to you to tell everyone else. The darkness seeped into Drake's life through his pride. It told Drake that He was doing more than God was. Lying to Drake and telling him he was doing everything for God and Drake was getting nothing in return for all his hard work, that it wasn't fair to Drake. Before he knew it or could realize what was going on Drake had soon turned against God and was planning to take His throne from Him. The darkness had taken Drake's heart from God. Evil is always waiting for its chance to steal your heart from God too. Always seeking. Always crouching.

Chapter Seven:

Chapter Seven: Heaven Proclaims

7

Heaven finally had all twelve dragons in their assigned positions. There was Drake, one of the original first dragons to serve. Angelina is a leader and a servant, who could fade into the spirit realm. Ziggy, is a playful caregiver for the kids and children who went to Heaven. Alexander, another leader and administrator serving God. Eight other dragons serve with them. Toshi, Orion, Adriana, Jasper, Pharamond, Raphael, and Samuel. They also have great testimonies, but we will learn about them another day. This is the current League of Protectors. They were all here; assigned to their stations. Each dragon has a spot on the city's wall that surrounds the perimeter. Each dragon has a portion of the wall and a section of humans that they are responsible for. They were clothed in God's Armor when they were honored. Their scales were covered in an impenetrable gold diamond that reflects the flow of God's Light further onto the Earth; keeping the darkness from entering into Heaven.

Heaven is a place free of any darkness. God's Light fills every inch of every position that there is. God and His Son, Jesus radiate a pure light that fills everywhere. Gleaming through the streets and overflowing over the edges of Heaven down onto the Earth onto His people. Nourishing their spirits. No darkness can live where there is so much pure light filling a place. Heaven is for all Light Bearers. It is their reward when their mission on Earth is done. There will be no more sorrow, tears, or pain. No more anxiety, worry, or fear. No more hate, anger, frustration, or doing without. Heaven is a place where people can be at peace. He has created for us a city. A city gleaming like pure gold; almost transparent like glass. Nothing dirty or unpure will be allowed to enter the gates to get into Heaven.

The city is big and its gates are made from one pearl. Glimmering in the light. There is a river of the Water of Life that flows down through the center of the city from the thrones of God and His Son; the Lamb of God. The water flowing in the river is as clean as you can imagine. Shining crystals of the purest water you have ever seen. Beside the River of Life is a huge tree. Its branches are old and strong. The leaves are healthy and thick. Its shade is cool and there is always a light breeze rustling through the branches. It bares twelve different kinds of fruit. One fruit for every month. Never sleeping or taking time to wither. It is always full of life and producing good fruits. This is known as the Tree of Life. The leaves of the tree were for healing the nations. God is the source of all healing both spiritually and physically.

Those who have a relationship with God understand this best. Their relationship with Him has proved to their minds and their hearts that the only way to make sure your light shines bright is to stay so close to Him. The weight and burdens of the world bash your body and soul like driftwood floating too close to the cliffs. The waves of evil are pounding us against the rock with every attack of the enemy. It feels as if there will never be an end to the abuse we take. From nature. From time. It's never-ending. It's almost more than we can bear. Then God comes into our life and shows us that we don't have to submit to the beating of this world. Through Him and His Son's sacrifice on the cross, we can choose to get out of the water and live life without bondages and fear. When God shows us that there is a better way to live through these attacks we become transformed into a new creature. We could never go back to living in yesterday's mindset of when we were constantly being abused. We will never go back to that ever again. Because of the freedom that we have experienced, our worship changes. Our lives have been changed. Our loyalties have been changed. Our friendships change. Everything changes to reflect the good that has been done in us.

In the center of the city is God's Throne Room. Around His Throne, there are twenty-four elders who are bowing and giving God their crowns of gold and silver to the only Living God. There are four living creatures serving God day and night. There at the feet of His Throne are great multitudes of angels and humans singing God's Praises. Their worship is unlike any other sound on Heaven or Earth. God says that the sound that is made out of great humbled gratefulness and thankfulness can only come from the freedom that is being released from the bondage created by darkness and evil. When you realize He has saved you, it is then your true worship can come forth. When you realize you are free, your body and feet can't help but dance. When you realize that you no longer have to carry the burdens that the world demands that you carry, your spirit man, your soul, and your body can worship in complete unity. From that unison comes the sound of triumph can be released. That is the worship of Heaven and it can only come from giving us free will.

The world takes its toll upon a person. The burdens of carrying the emotional and the physical responsibilities can wear on the body. We can only be healed by being in His Presence. When one goes to their secret place to sit with Him and worship Him they find themselves coming out renewed and refreshed. But we also come out knowing His Wants and His Heart better. It is the same with any relationship. You must sit and talk to each other to get to know them better. You must communicate with them your feelings and thoughts. You must tell them about things that you are going through and how those events are affecting your life. Communication is important in any relationship. But for you to grow closer to God it is vital to talk to Him. That you share with Him. You need to tell Him how things or events make you feel.

However, even though communication is important, so is listening. You may ask God how to get to Heaven but if you don't listen or hear His answer, then what was the point of it all? Listening to His Heart is the only way you will get to know who God is and what He expects of you. He is always talking to us and our questions are always answered. We may not understand His answers or what they mean, but they are the answers nonetheless. That's where our faith truly is tested and comes into play. It's through our faith that we trust in Him. It is our testimonies of the truths we have learned and experienced that will tide us over until we understand what He is talking about. We just have to be patient and wait for Him to reveal more of the details to us. If we fall into the temptation of sin or believe the lies from the darkness we can lose our ability to be close to God and the further we get from Him the softer His voice gets.

I would imagine that the further The Fallen Ones got from God would have disabled God's ability to speak into their lives, but I have always wondered if The Fallen Ones felt God pulling away. If they felt their Light diminishing as if someone covered their candle with a basket. Suffocating the nourishment it needed to glow. Was there a seed planted of discord and hate that began to grow and pull them away from Him? What happened to the goodness that flowed from God into their life that caused them to sin so greatly that they were eventually banished from Heaven? What could they have done to be disowned by the Father God? We had always been told that nothing could tear us away from His Love. No height, no depths, no chasm too wide that could keep us from His Love. His Love was like the air we breathe. It was vital to our very existence and yet The Fallen Ones chose to live without Him. I would imagine that if we could talk to them now they might show great signs of regret and shame. One can wonder…

~ * ~

There was something about rolling over and opening your eyes to God's Glory for the first time. A magnificent dream you don't want to wake up from. Everything is perfect. The weather, the sounds, and even the breeze seem to make you smile. Alexander looked around not realizing yet what had happened to him. He knew something was wrong but the details weren't quite clear in his mind. He felt in his heart that he should be sad but the glow that surrounded him made it hard to be. He felt the loss, something was missing but he couldn't find the memory to tell him what. He knew he should be angry but didn't know why. He touched his forehead but quickly realized his scales were covered in a hard material on his head. There was a warm glow that flowed through him. He felt different. He felt stronger. His eyes could see further and clearer. He could breathe deeper than ever before.

Before he could figure out where he was, he was called in his spirit to the throne room. Somehow he knew where that was. He saw it in his mind and as he saw it, his spirit body started floating toward the upper cascades to a higher place than he was. As he was moving closer to the center of the falls he sensed that he was moving toward a purpose. For the first time, Alexander was moving towards the reason for his life. He knew in his heart that he was about to meet his creator and he took a deep breath as he entered His Courts.

His Presence thickened as Alexander got closer. When he entered the throne room and was standing before God and His Son, Alexander was immediately humbled by the sight of them. Alexander's eyes teared up and he laid his head upon the cool floor before him. As his head lay on the floor, he couldn't help but think how he wished Baldwin were here to see Him with his own two eyes. Baldwin— he remembered Baldwin, Annabeth, and the boys were in danger. He remembered their faces in great detail. He could still hear Baldwin's voice guiding him. That was the whole in his heart that he felt. He was missing his friend. He felt peace come because he knew that he was in the presence of God Almighty. There was no greater reward than this. He and Jesus began to speak to Alexander as if they were long-time friends. They knew him and his life. They spoke to him about the good things he did and the glory that Alexander brought God. Alexander hung his head. He felt unworthy of any praise for the good things he had done because he never knew why he did them. He just felt led to them like a moth was drawn to the fire.

God explained to Alexander that he was drawn to do good because He had created him to do good. Not bad. He explained that He had created everything to be good and to glorify Him but that the darkness came in the night and distorted some that were weak and asleep. The darkness caused the Light Bearers to turn away from the Light and even though God can not intervene because of their free will, He still loves and cares for them. He is always calling them to Him; guiding them back to the Light.

God walked with Alexander for what felt like hours. He talked with him about what God's plans have been for the twelve dragons and their stations. How each dragon was strengthened and gifted to serve in their specific gift for a specific purpose. Their single purpose is to protect Heaven and humans from the darkness. To spread the Light everywhere. Each dragon's set of gifts is unique to them and their experiences. No testimony is the same because no life was lived the same. Therefore their testimony could be used differently according to their purpose. For some, their gift was to share the gospel; the good news about the goodness of God. For others, their gift is to discern between good and evil. Because sometimes it's not easy to tell if there is a difference. Deception has a way of manipulating anyone or anything it can to get his way. The one who is deceiving will lie to no end to make sure you are caught in his trap. The darkness wants what it wants and will use anything necessary to accomplish its goal. That's why the gift of discernment is so important. God gives us the ability to know the truth through Him and to see one's intentions. However, if used by someone corrupt…then we have a tale.

Ziggy carried the gift of discernment. He was Drake's first and easiest accomplice. Since he was one of the newest to come into the League of Protectors it made manipulating him easier. For he was not aware of all the significances of Heaven. At first, he did not know what he was getting involved with when he began to spend more time with Drake. I'm not even sure that Drake knew what was truly the heart of the matter when they began to talk. It started innocently enough. Drake was mentoring Ziggy and teaching him the responsibilities of a dragon in Heaven. But the more time they spent together the more comfortable Drake became with his complaints and grievances. Ziggy became a tail chaser. Everywhere Drake was, there was Ziggy close behind him. Always following him around and always doing meaningless tasks for Drake.

Before our eyes, two of our very own beloved were turning away from us. Turning away from everything they once stood for and held so dear to their hearts. They managed to convince themselves that they were a formidable force that couldn't be reckoned with. Their heads and bodies were carried differently. They walked with pride and an arrogance that was not who God had created them to be. There is a difference between having humble pride because you are happy with who you are and having a selfish nature trying to justify who you have become. There is a clear separation of the feelings you leave with those who look upon you after the darkness has seeped into your soul. You either leave people feeling happy and full of joy that they had an encounter with you or you leave them feeling like they just got dipped into a vat of greasy black oil and they can't get clean fast enough after you have left. There is a sadness that you left in their soul for the ones who knew you before the darkness got you. They miss who you used to be. They long for the joy you brought to their hearts. They're sad and they don't know how to get you back.

That's how we felt when Ziggy turned from us. He used to be so happy and without a care in the world. Happy with his children; playing with them and making them laugh. He used to have a bounce in his step that made him almost appear like he was trying to dance or skip as he walked. Now his steps are heavy with the weight of the world bearing on him. He stopped meeting with God in his secret place. He no longer spoke of His praises and sang His songs in his heart and it showed. He was a different dragon. He was no longer a joy to encounter but a memory of a childhood stolen by the night.

~ * ~

Alexander was not as easy to turn away from God. It took the darkness a lot longer to reach Alexander's heart. His heart's foundation was tied to his love for Baldwin, Annabeth, and the boys. His foundation of love for God had experiences and joys that were built by the relationship with Baldwin. Every good thing that Alexander had was sealed in his memory of the good seeds Baldwin had planted in his heart and mind. The joy that was in the memories that they had together was everything to Alexander. It gave him a reason to wake up in the morning because he longed for the day that they would join him in Heaven and they would be together again. He couldn't wait to see them laugh and smile when they saw how radiant he was now in Heaven. He was no longer dark and dirty. He was clean and as white as snow. His scales were now white and they reflected a warm golden glow. He was happy with who he was in God's Kingdom. He had a purpose in helping God take care of Heaven. He loved keeping things organized and leading others to do the same. He loved that he could interact with all the humans that came to Heaven. He loved that he could talk, guide, and encourage them to continue on their righteous path. It was nothing like his life on Earth where he was always worried and in fear of what could happen in the future.

In Heaven, he was important and he felt that he could do anything. Having a relationship with God gave him the freedom to follow his heart and to do good like he always wanted to do on Earth. His only sadness was the whole he felt missing Baldwin and his family. Quite often Baldwin found himself in the gardens by the river thinking about them and how wonderful it would be to have them here in Heaven with him. That's where Drake came into Alexander's life... Drake noticed one day that Alexander spent a lot of time sitting by himself and just thinking as he stared off into the river or the sky. He walked up to Alexander and asked him if he was okay. Like a fox climbing into a vineyard and stealing all the good grapes, Drake came in and stole Alexander's joy through his heart for Baldwin. The darkness came in and made up lies about the situation that were not true. "God didn't want you to be happy. That is why He took you from them and Baldwin is just going to get into trouble again. Only this time he won't have you to save him." The lies the darkness spoke to Alexander's mind disabled his ability to see the truth.

Because Alexander didn't take control of his thoughts and he didn't ask God for His Help, the darkness was able to turn him away from God and The Light to do good. In doing so, Alexander spent more time away from God. He still went and took care of his chores but the time He had set apart to spend with God became less every day he listened to the lies. He gave that time to the darkness, thinking about the past and the pain. Contemplating its truth when he knew in his heart it was a lie. The pain in his heart that longed for Baldwin's friendship to be in his life again became heavier than Baldwin could bear until one day he decided that going back to Earth to be with Baldwin again was more important than who he was to God. It was then that the plans Drake had conjured became Alexander's. All he wanted was to see his friends again. All he could see was the greatness of the powers he had on Earth. All that he could feel was the good he did in his past for Baldwin and his reward was being honored by going to Heaven. But when Alexander set his mind on the past he became his own worst enemy. Allowing the darkness to pull him away from God.

~ * ~

Every day was a beautiful day in Heaven. The birds were always singing. The Light was always bright and warm. The River was always clear and shining. The Tree always had fruit on it. True friends could always be found. This is where Angelina found a home. She had friends; both human and dragon. She had God as her guide and provider. She was a leader and a servant like she always was. She was a good and faithful servant on Earth. She led thousands of humans to safety. However, her path has always been a lonely one. She never had friends or the passion of a lover. She grew old never knowing the touch and taste of either. She was honored to be who God needed her to be. But she was so alone when she met God that day in the cave. She grew up not having anyone there to love her and care for her. When she appeared in that cave, she found a friend that she never knew she needed or even wanted. Every day since she has been returning the love that He gave her that day. In Him, she felt like she had a family again. In Him, she knew she was loved. In Him, she felt complete.

In Heaven, she continued her passion. Only in Heaven, she is surrounded by friends. She found dragons who cared about her and were honorable in their actions and with their words. They were dragons she could be proud of. Not like the dragons she had relationships with on Earth when she was a young dragon. They were always looking to cause trouble and death everywhere they went. The dragons in Heaven were helpful and caring. She learned through those healthy relationships what God wanted and needed from her in Heaven. She learned from them that she could continue being good and honest and not be condemned for it by the other dragons because they too were on the same quest. It felt good to be a part of something bigger than just her. She was part of an elite group of dragons and angels who served the one true living God. She liked that in Him, in God she was chosen and highly favored in everything she did.

At least that is what she thought when she first started hanging out with Drake. Originally she thought his interests were those for her heart. Which sparked something new in Angelina. She had longed for love for so long but was never willing to chase after it. She always thought that if a dragon wanted her heart he would have to make his intentions clear. There shouldn't be anything hidden in his motives or actions. That he should be pure in his wants. With Drake, he was such a mystery to her. He was always so attentive to helping her and guiding her; that was his job. To make sure that she knew how to be a good dragon. But his stares told her that he wanted something different. His tail always seemed to lay close to her, almost as if it wanted to wrap around her. Or so it seemed. Was she just imagining things? Seeing things the way she wanted them to be but not as they truly were? Was the longing she felt for the connection, for true love, making something out of nothing? She ached to know the truth. She chased after the truth.

Angelina had created a false sense of reality that she and Drake would one day be in love. Her thoughts ruled her heart. She gave them all her concentrations. Any truth of God's plans for her soul mate lover was pushed away. It didn't matter that He knew that she longed for love in a soul mate because He did know. He had plans for her future. Plans for good and everything she could have ever asked Him for in a mate but she can't concentrate on anything but Drake. She had longed so hard for his love that she became obsessed with what it could be. If Drake would only open his eyes and see her standing there. She stayed by his side and built him up regardless of the evil he had done. She had a way of justifying the bad for the greater good. The other dragons could see the chains the darkness was placing around her heart and no matter how they tried to tell her that it was not God's will and to reason with her. It only pushed her closer to this fake image of her and Drake. The more she thought about him the worse it got. She became consumed by his existence.

Drake's presence made her malleable and he used it every chance that he could. Hoping that her skills as a leader would come in handy once he got all the other dragons on board with his plot for the throne. Having Angelina following him would make it easier for the other dragons to see his perspective on how things should be run. He had all these wonderful plans for the power he would have once the takeover was through. He began to think about what he was going to say to the other dragons to sway them to follow him. He had this idea of how they could raise gold in a fundraiser to pay the dragons for their service to protect them. Humans would have to pay for their protection against the darkness. He would maintain the dragons to keep his realm safe from others trying to take it over; like a private legion of dragons that would be serving him on the throne. He plotted what he was going to say to tear his opponent down. How pushing God down would lift him above all others to be the only logical choice to lead them. He imagined himself sitting on the throne, controlling the universe, and keeping it in order. He could see and hear all the praises of all the humans and angels singing, glorifying him like they do God.

The humans would write poems and songs about how great he is. Once he overcame God and took Heaven for himself.

Drake knew what Angelina wanted from him but had no intentions of giving it to her. But he loved that she thought so highly of him. It gave him a power rush when she doted and longed for him. Her attentions although romantic still fed his pride. The power he had over their relationship caused him to crave the night. Before he knew it, he began to wonder how he could manipulate and control others to do his will. The thoughts engulfed his mind. Every move he took became a step closer to his endgame. The darker his thoughts became the more the night called out to him. The darkness called him into the shadows with every cruel intention. In every horrible plot, he said the darkness claimed a piece of Drake's soul pulling him further away from God. With every twisted plot, every hurtful word spoken dragged him further from the truth. All Drake could think about was the rush he was going to get seeing God come down off His Throne. Further away from the Light he ran. Because God has given us free will to live life however we see fit, all God could do was sit back on His throne and grieve.

~ * ~

God watched, as all four of His Protectors were succumbing to the darkness. No matter how many times He tried to reach out and talk to them, they continued to turn away from Him. He would knock but they wouldn't answer. He could hear the shame in their excuses when they would tell Him they would see Him later and He could feel their distractions building a wall between them. With every attempt that God made to draw them closer to Him, there was an equal or greater force pulling them away. Every thought God had for them was more than the sands in the sea. He wished that they could see the evil for what it truly was. He wanted to shield them from harm, but they pushed Him out of the way and ran straight into danger. He wished they could see what He could see in their future. He wished they could see the trouble they were walking into. But no matter how He would try to turn them around to come back to the Light, they rebelled back into their own distorted, manipulated paths.

He had his ideas on how to get their attention and their loyalty. He could use some of the ways that He used to reach humans on Earth. He could talk to them through a burning bush or He could have a creature come out of the river and swallow them like He did when Jonah wouldn't stop running from Him. He could ask a couple of the people in Heaven to go to them and tell them their story from when they lived on Earth. Or He could take their voices until they realized they had to come and talk to Him like He did with Zechariah during Elizabeth's pregnancy. But these dragons would see through the magic and know that it was God. He feared it would only push them further away from Him.

With the humans and dragons alike, He can always try to show them the way. They were created to serve, love, and be loved. Their life was built on the free will to choose which master they wanted to serve. They could choose to live to do God's Will which leads to freedom, happiness, and purpose or they can serve the darkness, which always leads to their death. He could try to intervene but ultimately it is always their choice. He promises them eternal life and peace in Heaven as their reward but to these four dragons, it wasn't enough. In their mind and their hearts, they still longed for something more. Even in Heaven, the darkness has baited them to need more. God knew their thoughts and their hearts. He continually provides for their future. For Ziggy, Alexander, and Angelina God could answer their prayers. Ziggy longed for a friend to value him and need him. Alexander needed Baldwin, Annabeth, and the boys back in his life. Angelina wanted someone to love and care for her romantically. God knew these prayers and wants. He could answer each of them, eventually. If they could be patient and wait for Him to provide.

However, He could not give Drake what he wanted. Ever. God knew Drake would come to the same conclusion and that would lead them into war. Drake would never be able to achieve the greatness that God can because he is not God. You can't beat, order, or demand someone worship you the way God is worshiped. Drake could never understand that.

Chapter Eight: No Savior

8

There is a war always around us. A battle for souls. The darkness has raged a war against The Light since the beginning of time. It has claimed creatures on all sides of the world. Our stories and the legends we have told our young ones speak of the war and its ability to affect our bloodline. Some bloodlines fight the same evil over and over until one chosen generation has had enough and breaks the chains off of their life. Stopping the evil right in its tracks and leaving it running in the opposite direction; licking its wounds and whimpering. But like a wolf pack trailing a man with a bad cut, the curse that once held a bloodline captive, is now looking for a way back into your life. Keeping its ever-watchful eyes on your every move; hoping that you'll let your guard down or fall away from The Light and give in to your temptations. The darkness is always looking for a way to make you ineffective in the war, but The Light is always there to fortify you and strengthen you. To protect and heal you. The two sides are always there. Waiting for your answer.

That's where The Fallen Ones have found themselves. In their secluded quiet space, trying to decide on which path they wanted to take. They could feel the darkness pulling and weighing on their decisions. Individually they all felt the strain evil was playing on their minds and bodies. But The Light carried them through each day and through all they were responsible for. It carried Alexander through his tasks making sure all the dragons were where they needed to be and held his attention focused on making sure everything went smoothly despite the drag he was feeling because he wasn't sleeping well. It held Ziggy as he received and took care of little children as they came to Heaven and weren't allowed to go home. The Light carried him as he distracted them to joy and led them to peace. Even though he didn't want to be happy. He wanted to go back to bed pull his tail around him and go back to sleep. He didn't know why he felt this way because he usually was pretty outgoing and happy. Ziggy began to notice he wasn't feeling like himself here lately. The Light even surrounded and carried Angelina moving forward as she led her groups throughout the Heavenlies. Angelina's thoughts were distracted and her answers were short. She didn't feel like talking too much. She just wanted to be left alone.

If the darkness can get you separated from those who love you and alienate you from others to keep you from being encouraged, then he has you right where he wants you. Primed to do whatever he wants you to do. A little whisper in your ear and he can manipulate you however he sees fit. Drake had become the very danger he warned his students not to become. The darkness wants you to become the very one who lies, manipulates, and makes others justify their ugliness to the world. If evil can get you to drag others down with you into the mud, then he has exploited you.

That's who Drake had become. He started listening to the darkness in his mind getting out of control and getting further away from God. Once the darkness had him alone, it began to use Drake's loneliness to draw others to his cause. He began by exploiting others with their faults and needs. Drake knew each of the dragons he had befriended had weaknesses that he could use to break them down and convince them to join him in his efforts against the Lord. In his alone time with each of them, he would say things like, "You know it was God who took you away from your friends." Or "Why would God want you to have friends so He can have you all to Himself?" He would manipulate the good that God was doing in their lives and turn it into darkness. Once this downward spiral into the darkness had begun, there was nothing God could do.

~ * ~

Drake woke up and it wasn't like any other day. This was the day he planned on confronting God. He wanted to show the others that the things that Drake was telling them in their alone time were true. Drake was going to show them that God didn't really care about the things that they did. He wanted to drive a wedge between them and God. But the one thing Drake never took into consideration was the seven things that the Proverbs tell us that God hates. Haughty eyes, a lying tongue, hands that shed innocent blood, a heart that devises wicked schemes, feet that are quick to rush into evil, a false witness that pours out lies, and someone who stirs up conflict in the community. When Drake woke this morning he carried all of them but the shedding of innocent blood. They were in Heaven, the humans and angels had already passed away and were in their spirit form. Several dragons had also passed away and were fortified in their spirit forms in Heaven. Dragons like Alexander and Angelina. But others were like Ziggy and had been promoted up to Heaven to serve in their real bodies. But it was never Drake's intention to kill someone during his takeover. But the day was still young.

Drake needed a reason for God to call him into the His Throne Room. For without God calling on you to come to Him, it is impossible to get into the Throne Room without an invitation. So Drake spent most of his free time that morning trying to figure out a clever way to get God to call on him. The darkness made him think he needed a plot to talk to God. Forgetting that all Drake had to do was call on God and he would come to him. But that wasn't good enough for Drake. He wanted to confront God in front of all the praising humans and angels. If he could convince God's worshipers to think less of Him then he would already be inside the Throne Room when they would take God off His Throne and give it to Drake. In his mind, it was the perfect plan. In his mind, people and angels were so easily manipulated. In his mind, this was the perfect way to take God out of his way.

~ * ~

Ziggy woke up and was a little more excited than he had been in the last few months. Something about today felt promising and new but he had yet to figure out why. He went to sleep last night thinking about his new friend, Drake, and how they had so much in common. He liked talking to Drake. He felt like he was the older brother that Ziggy never had growing up. They were always laughing at silly things and silly stuff others were doing. Drake mentored Ziggy and taught him how to think about things like an older dragon would. Ziggy looked up to Drake. At first, it looked like mutual respect between the two friends but the more you watched it became almost more like a form of emotional abuse. Drake started off picking on Ziggy by saying things like, "You ding dong. How can you think like that?" to saying things like "How stupid can you be? You're such an idiot!" What started as playful brotherly banter turned into a form of verbal and emotional abuse against him. It became painful to listen to and watch. It wasn't right how he was being treated. Ziggy's friends couldn't talk to him about it. He would defend Drake no matter what you would say about the hurtful things being said and done to Ziggy. Ziggy would justify that it was okay and that they were just playing around. That's how Drake showed Ziggy his love.

The night before, when Ziggy was thinking about his friend he couldn't help but think about the way Drake was talking and treating him. Sometimes the things he said were a little harsh but that's how Drake was. He was a rough around-the-edge type of dragon. That's how friends treat each other, right? You can't take anything your friends say to you personally. They were just joking around. They didn't mean any harm by it, right? Ugh, but then why does it make him feel so bad about himself? Why did he feel so icky? Most of the time when Drake said those things he would just laugh and play along but deep down inside, his heart was hurt. He was trying to go to sleep but he was frustrated with it all and he had decided to talk to Drake about it tomorrow when he saw him. He was trying to go to sleep but he was agitated. He was tossing and turning for what seemed like hours. He finally went to sleep because he asked God to help him go to sleep. He slept all through the night and he was feeling refreshed when he woke. When he woke feeling so good about life he had convinced himself that he was overreacting to the situation about Drake. So he decided that he didn't need to talk to Drake about it any longer.

However, as the day moved forward Ziggy was getting increasingly agitated over the smallest things. Things that shouldn't have bothered him at all. Too embarrassed to talk to God about it and too ashamed of his feelings to ask for his friends' opinions. He just stuffed all the negativity and hurt emotions deep down inside his soul. Which brought all those icky feelings right back up to the surface.

Ziggy was in a horrible place and he knew it. But he had a job to do. Drake expected him to get things done for the little ones and he couldn't let him down. He became a quiet festering time bomb waiting for the right spark to set him off. It was only a matter of time.

That's when Pharamond, the Protector of Journeys, came to talk to Ziggy about what he was seeing from the outside. He knew something was going on because his gifts were pulling him to Ziggy like the pull a moth has to a flame. Pharamond was another one of the dragons who were chosen in life to ascend into Heaven without suffering through death. His gifts were in Leadership and Pastoral Leadership. He led many other dragons to come to know the Lord in his lifetime. Through his gift as a pastor, he has also the gift of Discernment of Spirits. So it took some time but after a while Pharamond found Ziggy to be the common denominator to all the shadows that had appeared in Heaven in the last few months. So when Pharamond asked Ziggy to sit down in the garden with him to talk, Ziggy was already primed for an argument. Ziggy tried to get out of the conversation by saying he was too busy to talk right now. It wasn't a lie. Ziggy did have stuff he had to tend to but he could sit for a few moments and talk with Pharamond. Pharamond followed Ziggy through the courts insisting they talk. Pharamond pleaded with Ziggy to slow down and breathe, but Ziggy kept walking to get to his next task.

With each step and with each plea, Pharamond never let up. Chasing after him to stop and talk to him. Ziggy only got angrier at him for pushing so hard. He didn't want to talk about his bad feelings. He didn't want to deal with all the emotions suffocating him right now. He just wanted life to go back to normal. He wanted to be happy-go-lucky Ziggy again and he didn't know how to get him back. He didn't know what had been done to him to make him so angry all the time. He just knew that he wasn't himself. He just wanted them all to go away and leave him alone. But the discernment in Pharamond's Spirit would not release him to leave. It only got stronger. The worry and the love in Pharamond's heart wouldn't let Ziggy go. Pharamond kept seeing Ziggy running towards a cliff and he was going to fall off to his death if he didn't listen to him. Pharamond had to do something to get Ziggy to stop running away from him. In his frustration, Pharamond reached out to Ziggy's arm and screamed at him, "Stop Running Ziggy!"

At that moment, Ziggy's temper got the best of him, and like a loaded oil tank, his rage and his anger exploded. When a dragon's intense emotions are bottled up and then released into the universe, it tends to look like a power surge of cosmic radiation. Ziggy's emotions had been pushed down for several months and in that moment the piercing love that Pharamond displayed released all of Ziggy's emotions all at once. His fear. His rage. His anger was released with such a furious explosion that it killed Pharamond instantly. Ziggy stood there over Pharamond's body and when realizing what had happened he fell to his knees and began to cry. Raphael was another one of the league's leaders and he was on the other side of the courtyard with a class when Ziggy exploded. He ran to Pharamond's side and began to take care of him. He was a healer and he called his class to come help him take Pharamond to his healing station. Drake, Alexander, and Angelina were in the courtyard walking towards the commotion and screaming when it happened. They saw everything and in an instant, Drake's need to come up with a plot to get them all called to God's Throne Room was answered.

Drake realizing the danger that Ziggy was now in, ushered the three dragons to his cave to go over what they needed to say and do. Drake felt that if he left everything up to them, nothing would go as he had planned. Drake needed Ziggy to innocently somehow blame God for letting him get to that point. To say that he had been feeling neglected and left out of the activities that the other dragons were involved in. Ziggy needed to shift the focus off of himself and get everyone looking at God. However, Ziggy felt uncomfortable blaming God for anything. God had always been good to him. At least that is what he had always felt in his heart. He never felt God had any ill will over his life, but then Drake began asking them questions that had never crossed their minds before. Saying things like, "I can't believe God let your frustrations get the best of you like that. You know that's not like God to leave a dragon alone for so long. Do you know? Allowing bad emotions to get the best of us like that. I wonder what had God so distracted that He let Ziggy get so upset. I'm sure that he just must not care for Ziggy like He cares for the humans. I'm sure God has a reason for leaving him all alone like that."

It got Ziggy thinking about it out loud. "You know God does leave me alone a lot. He never pays attention to me like He does the others.

Maybe Drake is right. Maybe God doesn't love me as much as He does the other dragons. Maybe I am not good enough. Maybe I'm just too new and He doesn't have time to spend teaching me how everything works. I'm sure He has plenty of other more important things to deal with. Maybe it is God's fault. Maybe I am not worthy of such a position in Heaven. He shouldn't have promoted me so quickly. I must not have been ready for all these responsibilities yet. What was He thinking?!? It was His fault for bringing me up here." Which left Ziggy feeling defeated and unloved. Which left room in the other's minds to wonder about the same things in their thoughts.

They began to justify blaming all their faults and unlived dreams on God. They all in some way had a reason to be mad at Him. Alexander's life ended way too early. He wasn't ready to be away from Baldwin and his family. He never got to have a love or care of a lover. He never got to see his children or to have a family of his own. He never got to find out about his parents and his brothers. He never got to see what their lives had come to. He never got to see the world and see what he could do with his life. He had so much he had left that he wanted to see and people he wanted to help. He was supposed to be there for Baldwin and his family. He wasn't done yet.

Angelina's life wasn't what she wanted out of it. She wanted to be loved and to have a family. She wasn't through with all that life had to offer her. She wanted to see the world. She wanted to see the cliffs by the ocean. She wanted to see the volcanoes in the Pacific. She wanted to meet and live with the dragons in China for a few years, She wanted to fly up into the high cold mountains and see the people hike. She wanted to see the huge desert sands across the big seas. She had so much flying she never got to do. She had so much more that she wanted to do. Why did she have to come up here and continue with what He wanted from her? She never got to fall in love and be chased through the air by someone who loved her. She never got to see who her kids were and who they would grow up to be and how they would glorify God. Why would God take the opportunity for her to see that away from her? She sat in the corner across from Drake in the cave and mulled over these troubling thoughts.

Well, Drake, all his faults had to be God's problem because he could never be the reason for his downfall. He was created by God to work hard and to serve Him with everything that he did. But why? He should've been the one on the throne if he was going to be the one doing all the work. They should all be praising Drake. Every human and angel in the Heavens should be singing his praises. His throne would be higher than God's was. Drake sat back in the shadows of the cave and watched as the room lit up in a blaming God frenzy. Everyone was mad at God for how their lives turned out and none of them were happy about it. They wanted God to answer for it and Drake was going to lead the way to help them get their answers. God should be calling on them anytime now…

~ * ~

They waited for their call but it never came. God unexpectedly never wanted their version of the truth. He never called on them to know what they saw. He never asked anyone what had happened. That made everyone anxious. It caused the four dragons to worry. It made them all walk a little slower. They didn't know what was taking Him so long to call on them for answers. What was He waiting for? Every minute was spent waiting to address God for all the stuff He had done, or not done for or to them. But with each moment that went by only diffused their anger. But without their repentance, they would still be guilty. After a few more days of sitting quietly, Ziggy could no longer take the weight of the shame. He called out to God in his desperation and frustration. Sitting in the middle of the courtyard he called out God's name, "Yahweh! I need to talk to you!" There was no answer. No sound. No movement. Nothing. Ziggy called on Him again, "Elohim! Abba! Adonai!?" Still no response.

Was God there? Did He hear his cries? Why wouldn't He answer? Why did He not come to him? Could God see that Ziggy needed Him to answer his call? Ziggy waited for days. God never came to Ziggy. He never brought answers to all his questions. He never came to give Ziggy direction or support. Just the stillness of a peaceful universe void. He couldn't eat or drink. He just sat in the courtyard curled up on the small portion of grass where Pharamond had tried to help Ziggy. Where Ziggy lost his temper and caused a dear friend harm. A dark moment that robbed Ziggy of all his joy and happiness. The place where everything changed. The place where the darkness changed everything.

~ * ~

On Earth, the darkness can be best described as a thick black oil that spreads everywhere the host goes. One person can allow darkness to manifest in their spirit or their mind instead of taking control of their thoughts and submitting them to the Father, they allow it to grow. Turning into a contagious oil. You are angry because you didn't get the promotion you wanted and you start taking your disappointed grumpy attitude against your co-workers or you take it home and get upset with your wife and kids. Your wife is already having a bad day and she gets angrier because you just snapped at her for no reason. She takes that anger out on the neighbor kid who just accidentally knocked over her trash cans on his bike. He then has increased feelings of depression and rejection because of the divorce his parents are putting him through. He then starts to plan how he is going to kill himself because no one loves him or cares for him. All because one person didn't take control of their thoughts and feelings according to God's Word. At any point in time, any of those people could have stopped the oil from spreading to another. At any point in time, any of them could have chosen to say, "I must not have gotten that promotion because God has something better planned for my life. I will rejoice in my waiting. For He is good and He has great plans for me," or "Wow, my husband must have had a bad day. I will make him a great dinner to try and make it better. Kids, let us pray for Daddy to have a better day."

In Heaven, dragons can look down on Earth and can see the destruction that the darkness can so easily cause. Both in people and in dragons. As believers, we have eyes that can see the darkness and its plans for destruction to spread. Maybe that is why it is so important that we reflect God's Glory everywhere we go because the darkness is always trying to ruin the goodness in this world. That's why the story of The Fallen One's disgraceful acts has always bothered me. The records tell us that their pride led to their downfall and caused them to get cast out of Heaven but how could they let their pride get the best of them? Didn't they have ways to protect themselves from the darkness that could get into their minds? Weren't they spending time with God?

Talking to Him always helps me keep my heart and mind in the right place. I go to Him and let Him carry all my heavy burdens and my worries. Giving it all to Him allows me to release my anxieties and cares. Some of my worries don't go away and I am still a little worried but I leave Him feeling like I am no longer alone when I have to deal with whatever was bothering me. Spending time with God is vital to any dragon. It's the only thing that keeps us capable of reflecting His Light into all of the Earth. If we don't know who created us how can we effectively share with others His good works? If we don't spend time talking to Him and listening to His Answers then how can we share the Love that He wishes for us to show? If we don't know our maker how can we proclaim to serve His Purpose? Not effectively that is.

I have been roaming this Earth for thousands of years and it's always the same story. Someone hurt me and now I have to be angry, hurt, afraid, enraged because of what they've done…Then I have to take my anger or whatever other ugliness I am carrying and cause someone to hurt along with me. Hence the phrase, "Hurt people, hurt people." Well with my dragon brothers and sisters, it is no different. With the darkness, it is always the same oil spread. Unless someone goes to the only Living Water source to wash it off of them. He is the only water that can make us clean of any anger, rage, jealousy, pain, fear, anxiety, or pain the darkness has caused us. Spending time with God is the only way we can get clean and stay clean so that our goodness is pure and that our Light stays bright.

If I have learned anything in my thousand years, keeping a close relationship with God is one and the other is God cannot fellowship with darkness. He loves us with all His Heart but when we have partnered with the darkness, our relationship changes. It deeply hurts Him and saddens Him to keep us at a distance but He cannot have anything to do with someone if they choose to be a part of the very things that are hurting them. It's like there is some unwritten rule in the universe that keeps God from being a part of anything evil. He just can't. So when we choose to be a part of darkness, it breaks His Heart because we chose that over being with Him. We continue to repeat the same mistakes Adam and Eve made in the Garden of Eden when Eve listened to the serpent. God told them they could eat any fruit of any tree in the garden but not from the one in the center of the garden. That was the Tree of Knowledge of Good and Evil. God had given Adam and Eve everything they could have ever wanted. Endless lush living in the Garden of Eden, unlimited fruits and vegetables, and let us not forget to mention walking with God in the cool of the end of the day. They had the life most only dream of having. All they had to do was listen to His instructions.

Instead, they chose to partner with the darkness instead of listening to God. Breaking God's Trust with them and getting them kicked out of the Garden. They chose to live their lives separated from God and His Blessings to a life of hard labor and the hot sun. In everything, He always gives us a choice but with our choices, we always will have to let something go. So when Drake and Fallen Ones chose to walk in darkness they chose to walk away from God and His Love. God couldn't answer Ziggy even if He wanted to. Ziggy had just killed one of his friends. He was angry and enraged. The original law states that Light cannot fellowship with the darkness. Until there is a change of heart, God won't come anywhere near evil. Ziggy had to get away from his current emotions and thoughts. The only thing that was going to push Ziggy in the right direction was time alone. He had to spend some time thinking through everything that had happened and what he was going through.

Time always works in God's favor. The darkness uses your irrational emotions to manipulate you to move the way it wants you to, Quickly and recklessly. However, every good emotion you can experience only gets better with time. A new love, for example, if it is good for you then you will see the fruit it will bear in time. If you start dating a guy, hold off on the intimate parts; the kissing, or anything more until marriage. Any new love if they want to be with you for the rest of your life then they will have no problems waiting a little longer. However, if they are only focused on the physical nature of the relationship then they will become impatient for you to get closer intimately. Nothing good comes from going too fast…except maybe in a race. But in everything else be patient and think things through. That's exactly what Ziggy needed to do. He needed to be still and think about what was happening in his mind and heart.

So God left Ziggy alone to think about everything. Ziggy started from the beginning when he came to Heaven. He remembered being so humbled and honored to serve God. He could barely breathe because he was so excited to get started. He could barely sleep the night before. He got excited in his heart when he remembered this time in his life. But one of the things that happens when you think about how good it was in the beginning is that you realize that at some point something went wrong. Something or someone entered your life and brought the bad into your world without you knowing about it. Ziggy retraced his steps and realized that the one dragon that once brought him so much joy was also the one who brought forth sadness. He couldn't tell you when it exactly happened because there wasn't a specific time or event that Ziggy could remember the darkness entering their friendship. But Ziggy realized that the only one that could be connected with the darkness that now lay within him was Drake.

Not just in how Drake spoke to Ziggy but in how he ordered him around to serve him. The more he thought about their relationship the sicker Ziggy felt. How could he not see that the cause of all his issues was right in front of him the whole time? Drake has been causing all sorts of problems for Ziggy. His doubt, anxiety that he was not good enough for anyone, and even his fear of losing his friends were all because of things Drake would say under his breath around Ziggy. He felt horrible because the only reason he was in Heaven was because he wanted to serve God with all his heart and to give joy and happiness to the children again. They had lost so much and they were waiting for all their loved ones to come home to be with them in Heaven. He answered God's Call on his life to be the dragon he was created to be. He came to Heaven to fulfill that purpose. How could he be so blind? How could he let another come between him and God? After all that God had done for Ziggy. Ziggy was devastated about what he had done. He was ashamed of who he had become. He wasn't who God had created him to be.

How could he ever be forgiven by God? What was he going to do now? All of a sudden he felt like everyone knew. He felt their eyes staring at him all the time. The shame he felt inside was unbearable. He didn't know where to go or what to do. He didn't feel that he was worthy to be in Heaven anymore. He didn't think he should be tending to the kids anymore. He felt like everything he had done was not who God wanted to serve any longer. Under normal circumstances, he would go to Drake with his worries because he was the oldest dragon and he was their mentor serving under God. But given everything that has happened and Ziggy's feelings after his thinking, he didn't feel that talking to Drake was the wisest action to take. At that moment in time, Ziggy remembered Alexander. He was one of the leaders in the Dragon administration. He couldn't think of anyone better to go to with his thoughts on Drake and since God wasn't going to talk to him right now, Alexander was the next best thing.

~ * ~

Alexander was sitting on the side of the cliffs of Heaven watching people down below when Ziggy came and sat next to him. He wasn't really in a talkative mood right now. He was preoccupied with his own problems and feelings. He was still working on a way that he could convince God to send him back to Earth to care for Baldwin and his family. He couldn't understand why he was in trouble with God. What had he done to make God mad at him? He was just standing there in the courtyard when the argument with Pharamond and Ziggy happened. The River of Life waters were falling to the lands below and their whispers were calming to their minds as they sat together in their thoughts. The stream of water slid gently over the smoothed rocks of crystal laid in the stream bed. The grass was lush and green slightly bending in the cool breeze rolling across the courtyard field. Alexander was surprised that Ziggy could even sit still and be quiet at this moment. He looked over at Ziggy and observed the loneliness in his heart. He felt sad for him as he realized how rough the last few months had been for him. Meeting Drake when he got to Heaven, had to have been the best and worst day in his life. How the darkness must have brought him to the despair that exploded in the courtyard that day. Alexander couldn't help but mourn for him and feel his pain. Because he too felt the darkness that had come over his life. It was written all over Ziggy's face. Alexander's heart was breaking looking at him and turned back looking at the rushing water falling below. Tears of sadness rolled down Alexander's face as he began to pray to God for his friend. He laid his cheek on the top of Ziggy's head that was leaning against his shoulder.

"God, I know that you don't want to talk to me right now. I know that I must have upset you to keep you from me. But Lord, will you hear my cries for Ziggy? His poor heart is so broken and lonely. Hear my cry for him, God. I know you and only you can heal this pain in him. Come and see to his broken heart and mind. Bring him back to the joy and peace when he first came to Heaven, Lord." Alexander spoke to God in his heart and mind.

Ziggy never heard a word come from Alexander as he sat there listening to the falls below. Ziggy just sat calmly waiting for Alexander to say something to him, but nothing ever came. Just the stillness of the friendship that the two dragons needed. As Alexander laid his head against Ziggy, Ziggy didn't feel so alone. After a little while, he realized that he did have a friend here in Heaven after all. He had Alexander. He didn't need anyone to tell him that. He felt it in his heart. Ziggy felt a warmth cover over him and he fell asleep there peacefully. He curled up beside Alexander and closed his eyes in the afternoon dusk. Alexander was almost twice the size of Ziggy. So Ziggy felt safe and secure against his friend. For the first time in months, he felt like everything was going to be okay. Little did he know that the darkness of the night held a different plan for him.

Ziggy woke up and he was running away from something chasing him. He didn't know exactly where he was at but he knew that he was running through aisles of products on shelves. If he had to give it his best guess off the top of his head, he would say he was in a marketplace. All he knew was that something evil was chasing after him and was trying to hurt him. He was flying through the marketplace so quickly that the details were all blurry and unrecognizable. The aisles and the people were there but they were not important to Ziggy. All Ziggy wanted was to get away from this evil and to get to safety. He kept looking over his left shoulder to see where the evil was. It was always there; taunting him and laughing at him.

Saying things to torment him every time Ziggy looked over his shoulder.

"I am going to get you now." Ziggy would fly faster to get away.

"There's nothing you can do to get away." Ziggy would fly faster.

"No one is here to help you. To save you." Ziggy started to cry as he pushed through the wind.

"I will finally silence you. There is no one who can help you."

Ziggy cried out loud and screamed at him. "I am wanted!" The evil laughed under his breath and continued to try and scare Ziggy into giving up.

"No one wants you. No one loves you. You're a killer."

Ziggy was only hearing things the darkness wanted him to think about himself. The words being spoken were only lies that were attempting to label him as something he was not. He was not a killer. He didn't mean to hurt Pharamond. He didn't mean to get so upset at him. He didn't mean to go off like that. That was not who he was. He refused to give in to the torture. "I am not a killer and I am loved!"

Ziggy was getting angry and tired of this accuser and his lies.

Then he woke. He looked around and couldn't see anything. But he could hear the waters falling down onto the Earth. He could hear the stream rolling through the Heavens and he could hear the voices praising God in the Throne Room. The praises there never stopped worshiping the Lord. Why couldn't he see anything? There was no nighttime in Heaven. There was no darkness ever in Heaven. So why wasn't he able to see? He tried to get up. He felt like he was still lying down. But he couldn't get up. What was going on here? He closed his eyelids in frustration.

"What is the point? You can't get away from me." He was trying to get away from the evil again. He could feel the threat of him on his neck. He looked over his shoulder again. Only this time something was different. He felt threatened but he was not as scared as he was before. He continued to try and get away.

"You have no voice. No one wants to hear what you have to say." The threat pursued him.

In Ziggy's mind, he didn't feel that was true. When he talked, others cared.

"They only endure being around you, but they don't really want to be anywhere near you." The liar says.

Ziggy remembered hearing God tell him often that he was loved and that he had a sound mind. God told him that he was God's Chosen. He was loved. God loved him. He remembered God telling him that. "God says I am loved and that I do have something to say to help others."

"That's so funny! If He loves you so much then where is He now? Why isn't He here to help you?" the darkness laughed. Ziggy noticed that the monster that was chasing him was a draft of smoke led by an impression of fear for a face. It had no body. Only a blur of gray smoke followed off to the side trails of Ziggy as he flew. Ziggy closed his eyes.

Ziggy opened his eyes and there was nothing but darkness all around him. He couldn't see anything but again he could hear the river falling. He was back to reality. He was still unable to move from the lying down position. It was hard to breathe. He tried to move his neck but something was pinned against his throat. He turned his head to each side trying to find relief to make breathing easier. He tried to move his wings to feel what was up against his throat. He was on his back. His wings were under his body. He couldn't free them. He kept moving his neck back and forth. Whatever it was that was holding him was hard and heavy. He couldn't move it with his neck. It was strong; unbreakable. He realized as he was assessing the rest of his body that he could not move the lower half of his body. He was paralyzed from the neck down. He could feel his body but he couldn't move. He had to figure out what was holding him down. He didn't know why he couldn't move but his accuser's words were still repeating in his mind.

He wasn't those things. The lies that the accuser was spewing out at him were upsetting. Ziggy's frustrations were building up inside. It seemed like he was in a battle fighting for his life and every moment made him question the truth of the reality he was experiencing. He knew at this moment in time he could feel his body. It was tired and his chest hurt. He could feel his legs but they wouldn't move. He could feel his arms. He could move them and his claws were working but they were weak. His arms were heavy. He still could not see anything but he could hear. He tried to speak to yell for help but his throat hurt and he could barely make any sound. He moved his arms around across the ground and he could feel the water at the end of his claws. He was lying next to the river stream. He could feel the glass crystal stones in the stream bed. He used his claws and grabbed hold of as many stones as he could. He rested for a second then mustered all the energy he could to throw the stones to get someone's attention. He closed his eyes and threw them as hard as he could.

When he opened them he was standing in the darkness of the marketplace. The spirit of fear stood before him staring at him. They were standing still; no longer flying.

"I told you I would kill you today." The spirit said.

"There is no one that cares whether you live or die. You will die a nobody." Which immediately infuriated Ziggy. That was not true. God loved him. God raised him. God told him that He sent His Son to die for him on the cross. God loved him. Ziggy missed God. He missed talking to Him. He missed their talks and His ability to calm him down. He missed calling on Him when he needed help. He wished he had never met Drake and allowed the darkness to ruin his life. He wished that he could call on God now. He wished that he could call on the dragon protectors for help. They could defeat this spirit that was attacking him. They could get this heavy object off of him. God would know what to do.

"God doesn't want to deal with you. If He cared for you He would be here for you. Wouldn't He? Where is God when you need Him the most? Why hasn't He come to save you and help you? He doesn't care about you. You aren't important enough for Him to care about." The darkness thrust its ugliness at him in a last attempt to kill Ziggy's hopes.

"That's NOT TRUE! GOD! I need you! I'm sorry for what I have done. I'm sorry for letting the darkness in! God! Father, I'm sorry! Please forgive me!"

He opened his eyes and Alexander was still sitting next to him. His friend never left him alone. He had fallen asleep next to Ziggy. He could move his arms again. He stretched out his legs and realized he was free. His wings were no longer pinned under his body. The last thing he could remember was he had thrown crystals, hoping to get help. He sat up and looked around. He could see again. He was still by the River of Life. The water sparkled like it never had seen sunlight before today. Ziggy sat there thinking about what he had just been through. Thinking about the things that were said and the hurts that were spoken over him. Was it all just a dream? It felt like it was a dream in his mind but the pains in his neck and his wings told him something completely different. The pain in his body told him that it had happened. He looked around him somewhat afraid that the torment was not over. That the evil spirit of fear was not gone. Why was he free from being chased by it? How did he get away from the darkness? The last thing he could remember was he called on God to come and help him. To forgive him for the things he had done. Then his eyes were opened and he was free. God had set him free.

Chapter Nine: A Mind Manipulated

9

Drake sat on the opposite edge of the courtyard and saw Alexander and Ziggy sitting on the cliff side. The spirit of fear swirled up and coiled around Drake's neck as it spoke.

"Alexander and Ziggy are awake. Their eyes have been opened."

Drake scoffed as he snarled at the spirit's report. "The seed of darkness has already been planted. We'll let it take root and grow for a while. Once the fear has grown in his heart we'll have them back on our side again." Drake said as the spirit of fear smiled as evil pleasures ran through his mind. Drake's plans were not easily destroyed. Only delayed. Which worked in Drake's favor because he had to get started with his other plans before he could be stopped.

~ * ~

Angelina stood in the courtyard, speechless for a long time. She couldn't bring herself to leave. Pharamond was her friend. Maybe not a real close one, but a friend nonetheless. However, she sat there and still couldn't believe her eyes. Little, happy-go-lucky, playful Ziggy killed her friend. Little Ziggy killed someone in anger and frustration. Was that even possible in Heaven? Drake sat down behind her and pulled his wing around her shoulder. Surprised, she looked at Drake and placed her wing on his. Angelina found herself unsure of the future. She felt so dark and sad. She couldn't bring herself to ask any questions from Ziggy. So when Drake ushered them all back to his cave she was comforted that they were all safe and together. She had become rather close to them all and during these cloudy days, that's all she could ask for. That her friends were with her and that someone was feeling as sad as she. But as they were talking the sadness turned quickly into questioning anger aimed towards God.

It didn't seem right, but it was how they all felt. Upset with the many things that kept going unanswered. All three of the younger dragons had a lifetime of episodes they couldn't control and were even harder to overcome. Alexander had his whole life turned upside down when his family got captured. He lost his older brothers. He still doesn't know what happened to them. Then he chose to save Baldwin and his family. Only to lose them before he was done living his life. Well you know Ziggy's current problems and then there she is. Never feeling like she got to live her life. She wanted to explore the world, fall in love, and have kids. They all needed to know something and God was nowhere to be found. He wasn't answering any of their calls. Alexander and Ziggy left to deal with their struggles on their own. Leaving Drake and Angelina to themselves. Angelina was surprisingly happy to have some alone time with him. Maybe now she can learn more about who he is.

When they left the cave the air filled with an awkward silence. Drake realizing that it was his job to entertain Angelina since she was a guest in his home, asked her if she wanted more tea. Of course, she did. She wasn't sure she was ready to go yet. As he started warming the pot for more hot water, she began with idol chit-chat. It had been so long since either one of them had even thought about entertaining the idea of love in their lives. They almost weren't sure how to talk or react to each other's awkward disposition. Angelina wanted to know more about him, more about his past and serving God for as long as he had. She was intrigued by his age and wisdom. The more he talked about his time with God and his always-changing responsibilities in Heaven, the more she realized how he became so upset and angry with God. She always thought he was so mysterious and complex but when it came down to it his anger was nothing more than a reflection of where he spent most of his time and it wasn't talking with God or reflecting Him. It didn't matter to her. The longer she spent with Drake the more she understood him and she felt like they were one dragon. Angelina was drawn to the love in him that she never got to have on Earth. The days they spent together started to fly by and the more they learned about each other, the closer they became.

The world around Angelina disappeared in the cloud of his love. He was so caring and attentive to her needs. She would barely have to think about needing something when he would show up with the very need there in hand. It was almost like he could read her mind. She had always imagined true love was thought out and spontaneous at the same time. True love is what makes you feel like you're lighter than air. Floating through the clouds in a dreamy fog. But grounded in a new reality that is nothing like the lonely life you left behind. Seeing everything vividly like you're seeing it for the first time. Then all of a sudden all you can think about is the other's life more than your own. You wonder about all their likes and dislikes. You wonder if they like the same things as you or hate the same things as you. Out of nowhere, this other life has bumped into yours whether you planned on it or not. They are now intertwined with your life.

Whether Angelina knew it or not, Drake's destiny was now engulfing hers. His plans were becoming hers. His anger was hers. His future was now hers. The love that she had for him made her blind to her wishes and desires. She had unknowingly let them go and replaced them with his. Her service and dream to serve God with all her heart was no longer a priority. She found herself following after Drake and making sure that everything he wanted to be done happened without any problems. Angelina kept telling herself that Drake loved her, he just had a hard time telling her. She would tell herself that he loved her. He wouldn't be working so hard every day if he didn't love her. He said everything that he was working so hard for was for them. So that they could be together and they wouldn't have to work any in the future. He made her broken promises that he wanted to spend his extra time with her but he had stuff he had to do to get the job done. He promised that one day soon he would spend the day cuddling with her. But those days never happened. With every one of his broken promises also brought hurt and bitterness. Her love for him was there but her heart wasn't as happy as it once was.

Every time she turned around someone was asking her what had changed and what was going on in her life. They began burdening her with reminders that she wasn't doing her responsibilities in Heaven well. Telling her that Drake had consumed her and that she needed to put some space between them because she was blind to what he was doing to her life. But all she could do was brush off their weak attempts to break up their relationship. It was her and Drake against the world and they just don't understand the bond that they had. How could they? Their love was one of a kind. No one would understand the love that they had. So she dismissed their pleas and after a while, she began to lose connection with her friends altogether. She would make excuses that they really weren't her friend. That she was better off without them bothering her and Drake all the time. But then she found herself reminiscing on the days when he would bring her flowers from the courtyard. Or conversations that were their plans for their future. Not the plans for God's downfall. Anymore that was all he could talk about. How he was planning to spend more time away from her instead of his plans to be with her. After a while, it began to hurt, because with every conversation there was a reminder that something else was more important than her. It felt as if he was making these plans for his agenda and it no longer included her. The benefits he proclaimed would happen soon never got completed and they never seemed to involve her. When was he going to pay attention to her and care about the same things she cared about? When was he going to want the same things she wanted? She found herself wondering if she still loved Drake the way she once did. Was she just in love with the idea of love? Or was this even what true love should feel and look like? Because it wasn't at all what she had envisioned for her future.

When she was a younger dragon she thought love was selfless and always kind. Love made a way through hot lava and through tormenting winds to save her from danger. It would leap over crazy icy mountain ridges and torrential rainstorms to save her from the masked crusaders attempting to kidnap her. It would scale high towers to rescue her from evil kings and fight off armies of soldiers trying to entangle her in ropes and chains. It always saved the day. It always came through. It always made your dreams come true. Love was always true and wouldn't put themselves in a compromising situation under any circumstances. True love follows through on things they say they are going to do. But those were the fantasies that a young dragon placed her hopes in for her future. Even as she grew up she tucked those fantasies away in the corner of her heart. She was always looking for this dragon who wasn't a young girl's daydream but a real hero that she could love and be loved by. She had lived her whole life on Earth and never found a dragon who met her ideals of love.

Maybe that was why she never fell in love because he didn't exist. Even as she stares at Drake as he plots his next moves, she realizes he is nothing like her daydream. Was she just settling for Drake because she was tired of looking for her hero? Was he just at the right place at the right time? Did she fall for him just because he was there and willing to comfort her when everything happened with Pharamond and Ziggy? God always told her to be patient, that He was working on her soul mate. He just wasn't ready to come to her yet. He told her that he would be perfect for her and that he would be everything she had ever wanted in her mate. He always told her to be still and to still her heart. To wait for the right day to come to her. Not to be too quick to get something before it was time. But she was so impatient. She was sick and tired of waiting for him to come to her. At first, she thought that Drake was the one. But time has only disproved that theory. Or maybe he couldn't live up to her ideals of the perfect love. She knew who he was when they started this. Was it fair to him to ask him to change now?

Would he even be able to change his ways now? He was dead set on bringing God down. Could he be led back to the Light? Did Drake love her enough for her to bring him into the Light? Did she love Drake enough to try? They haven't been together long. They still haven't had their first kiss yet. She longed for the kiss but it never came. She began to wonder if the love she was seeing was only in her head. She kept telling herself he was just very old-fashioned. But after a while, she began to question their love altogether. Now every move was under a microscope. She found herself looking for him to touch her lovingly. Or to speak to her about his plans for their future. Quite honestly she was looking for any evidence that he felt the same way that she did about him. The more she looked the less she could find. Which left her feeling lonely. She felt like a fool. Everything she thought was love was nothing more than her imagination playing tricks on her heart. Or maybe the longing of her heart played tricks on her mind. Either way, she again was left feeling unloved and abandoned.

What was she to do now? She was entangled in Drake's plans to take over Heaven and now she didn't know what to do. She saw what the darkness had done to Ziggy. She felt the truth of it in her heart. When Ziggy exploded on Pharamond she knew where the darkness in his heart came from. You couldn't be around Drake and not feel that somehow the darkness had touched you. Or at least affected you in some way. She could only assume that what happened to Ziggy would happen to her as well. The darkness has already caused her to lose most of her friends and who knows what else. She knew one thing she had to do right away and that was pull away from Drake. She had to make sure that it wasn't obvious to Drake. She worried about the backlash from him but in all reality, she didn't think that he would notice her pulling away at all. It was times like these that she missed God. She missed His wonderful timely advice. He would tell her exactly what she needed to do here. The more she thought about it, the more she became concrete in her decision on how to deal with it. But she needed advice. Who could she turn to for advice? Normally she would turn to God but He is not answering her. She was all alone in her plight. God told her He was always there.

She remembered when God told her He had to leave for a while. He told her He was leaving her with His Spirit. It was then she found her inner counselor. It was in His Spirit she found her direct access to God whenever she wanted His Help. All she had to do was find peace in her heart and call on God's Name then start talking. He always answered her in her heart. That was when she found herself at peace even during decades of wars. She found everything she ever needed. She missed those days when His Spirit was with her, helping her. She found herself wandering in her mind to the days when God and she walked so closely. When His steps and hers were not separated. She longed for those days again. Even though she was on Earth in living flesh and blood she felt more whole than she felt today. She had great memories of her time on Earth. She recollected so many times when she was unsure which way to go in the mountainous terrain when she and a group were fleeing battles. All she would have to do was call on God in her heart and mind. He would always tell her the safe way to go. With God, she was always safe. Safer than she felt right now. It was then her eyes were opened. He was her true love. He has always chased after her and kept her safe. His Love was always there comforting her, and making her feel loved and needed. His Love made her feel complete. She never had to worry whether God's Love was real or fake. She knew it because He showed it. He spoke it. His kindness was always true...

She came back to her reality of the present moment. She had forsaken her first love. She was finally alone in her cave. She had left Drake's for the evening and in her thoughts walked to her cave. She stepped in and was home where she could be true to her feelings. She coiled up next to her fire and cried. Nothing could change the regret in her heart. The conviction she felt was like a heavy load of steel that had been laid on her back. "Oh Lord God, I am so sorry I left you for another. Oh God, my God I am so sorry for my thoughts against you." She cried out. "God, please forgive me. Oh Lord, hear my cries!" In the darkness in the corner of her cave, she felt the burden of her pains lift. She felt a warm blanket cover her as she drifted off to sleep. She knew she was no longer alone. She knew she was forgiven but she felt that the love had changed. She let out a deep sigh because she knew that there was a long road of recovery waiting for her in the morning. She knew she had disobeyed Him and repentance was only the first step of the many that were awaiting her. Angelina fell asleep knowing she was going to need her rest.

~ * ~

The darkness is always planning on clever ways to tear apart other's lives. Keeping them from their happiness. It wields its way through others the same way it has maneuvered through Drake to hurt others. That's all the darkness wants to do. Destroy your hopes and dreams. Steal your joy and peace. Kill your willpower so that it can get you out of it's way. It will tempt you with those very dreams to get you off the path that God has for you. If it can draw you away from God's Will for your life, then it will have one less believer to fight in the end battle. The darkness is here to take us out, one by one. The Light is here to keep us Holy so that we can walk with God again in the Garden of Heaven. The Light is here to purify us of the darkness that has stained our soul. Since the day when man was cast out of the Garden of Eden, we have not been able to be with God since that day. There is only one way for us to be purified of the stains on our souls and that is through a repentant heart. It is the only way back to the Father's Heart.

It is the only way that the ultimate sacrifice of His Love can mean so much to so many of us. We were born into a life of fire, hate, and anger. With the sole purpose of hurting others in the way we were hurt. We hurt deep inside and so we can only feel better if we hurt others? No, that cannot be the way it was meant to be. We were born in this life and we were brought into the Light. We were created to bear the Light. To share the Light with others. Our purpose was to glorify the Father in Heaven and glorify His Name. I read our history and it just makes no sense to me. How could our lineage go from being great protectors of God and the Heavens to the scourge of the Earth? How could four dragons bring down a whole legacy created for good?

I know I am a young dragon but I refuse to believe that it's my Heavenly Father's Will for me to become a dark killer like my real father wants me to be. I do not feel that can be true about who I am. That doesn't feel like who I am meant to be. I know what my ancestors want from me. I know they want me to be savage. But when I wake in the morning and set out for my day gold and fire are not the first things that come to my mind. To be honest, it was usually what was there to eat nearby. How could any dragon be so lazy to think that their only purpose in life was to hunt out all the gold and to be feared by every living creature amongst us? I could think of many other things that would be better than those things.

Alastair was a young dragon. His curiosity about dragon history was constantly pulling at him. He has made several trips to the High Court to read in the library and he spent many hours by candlelight reading about people in history and dragon history. His hunger to find out more about the purpose of his life and the meaning of his creation drove him every day. He has always been an observant dragon. He learned more by watching others than he ever did trying to figure stuff out on his own. Alastair felt drawn to know more about why he was created with every fiber of his being. It is what drove him to spend so much time with the chronicles in the library. When he wasn't in the library he was alone in the mountain cave thinking about what he had learned from the readings.

History was full of many descriptions of gods and idols throughout time who claimed to be the rulers of many things. There were gods of the sun to gods of the sea. After a while, people ran out of elements to make a god for and began making up gods of silver and gold to worship. I think that people would worship the devil himself if that meant they could be allowed to do whatever it is they want to do. If the law won't let you live in the sin you want to live in, then let's claim that there is another god that will let me sin the way they want. But from what Alastair could tell that is all they were. Made up false creations of statues and metals that people put their hopes and faiths into. They made these entities up to justify not listening to the one true Living God. The thought crossed his mind that might have been why Drake did what he did. He lifted himself to be greater than God. That there was no use for God in his life. He had justified it to himself that he could do everything for himself and there was no value in obeying God's Law any longer. Why obey a God when you could be a God yourself, right?

It appeared to repeat itself throughout history for people. They didn't like the way God was telling them not to do something or they weren't allowed to do something and they would blame God for their downfalls or mistakes so they would make their own rules and decide what they wanted to listen to and what they didn't have to follow. If they made the rules then there would be no one that they would have to be held accountable to. When man realized they could make their separate gods, it all went downhill from there. More hatred, lying, and the killing increased. Anyone could justify their sins because as long as it wasn't infringing on someone more powerful than you what harm could there be? It was their right to sin however they wanted to. They didn't believe in God so why did they have to listen to Him? Or if He cared so much for me then why haven't I seen Him or what has He done for me? There was always a line or an excuse to disobey.

It burdened Alastair's heart to hear people's reasoning for the disobedience. Couldn't they see that God was telling them not to do those things because it would hurt them? He read story after story from beginning to end and it was always the same excuse. "I didn't want to," so then they would profess "Who's going to make me?" attitude that has spread throughout history. But then there were some who turned and listened to God. They heard His calling and they answered Him. They would have a divine connection with God just like the chosen dragons did. They could hear Him and talk to Him whenever they wanted to. They had a relationship with Him and when they did what God wanted them to do they were blessed and prosperous. When they listened to His Advice it would always lead them to a victory or away from a great danger. Go always protected those He Loved. Alastair wondered what that would be like. How amazing it would be to have someone wise to talk to every day. To help guide and lead his emotions through every day. He wouldn't have to get angry because God would be there to help him through it. He wouldn't have to rob and steal because God would be his provider. He wouldn't have to be anything but who God wanted him to be. If he could find out who that was.

When he read the chronicles about Angelina and her testimony she says that in the very beginning, God and her would walk in the evenings. He would tell her all about every animal that He had created and why He created them. Each animal was very detailed and with purpose on this Earth. The whole world has a reason for living. Every molecule had a purpose. Even the smallest of ants had a job to do. Some animals ate plants and leaves to help break them down to keep the forest clean. Then there were animals who ate the dead flesh of other animals. Every living thing has a responsibility to the world and their genetic code was given to them by their creator; God. God made them to make the world complete. However, Alastair still hasn't found the reason for creating the dragons. He had been at the library for days and was growing weary. It was time for a break to the cave. His resting place.

Alastair reached the cave and was immediately relieved of his worries. He started the fire and coiled up beside it to rest. Of course, his body was tired, but his mind was still not done with it's train of thought. He hated that about himself. That he would keep searching and trying to find out the answers to his questions. He wouldn't truly stop searching until he was satisfied with the truth coming to the surface. He often thought his process felt like he was looking into a lake of muddy, dirty water and he was searching for clean water in the middle of all the mud. He knew the clean water was there. He could feel it in his soul. He just had to keep searching. That's how he felt about the answers to his questions regarding the meaning of his life. It was out there, he just had to keep searching for the answers.

As he lay coiled up by the fire, his heart wished he could have been one of them. One of the original dragons who could sit and talk to God and be on the League of Protectors. When he was younger, he would pretend he and his friends were in the league saving the people from the darkness. They would all have directions straight from the lips of God. God would give them instructions on how to save the day and of course, like the perfect little soldiers they were, they would follow them explicitly. Alastair was always fighting for good, which irritated his father. His father always made him feel ashamed to want to be the good guy. He was often told he was a disappointment. He had to learn to ignore his father and seek the truth in his life. That was why the cave became his safe place. It was more home to him than his real home with his dad. He was old enough to no longer live with his dad. Alastair's only wish was that he could have a father who wasn't so dark and destructive all the time. They could have a better relationship if that were not his way. But it never seemed to matter. The darkness was always there. There hurting whatever magic there could be between them. Until his father returns to the Light, they have no hope of having a relationship ever again.

Alastair notices his fire pit needs some wood and he gets up to tend to the fire. What Alastair doesn't know is that God is always with him. He hears his thoughts and his questions. He knows the things that Alastair longs for in his heart and He wishes He could make Alastair's dreams come true. But because of the free will God gives us all, He cannot change his father for him. He can't make his father want to be in the Light and want to do good in this world. God could no more change his father any faster than He could change Cain from being jealous of his brother Able. It is his father's choice to be that way and on both accounts, God is saddened. He can only sit by and watch as we choose to do the darkness' works instead of reflecting God's Light to the rest of the world. But there was nothing God could do to give Alastair the father he needed and wanted. God can see all of time and He knows what is in our future. He knows what the darkness will throw at us and He does everything He can to provide, care, and keep us from harm. In Alastair's case, it was best to let Alastair continue alone, for now, in his research of the dragon and human history.

Alastair longed to not be alone. He dreamed of armies of others who were just like him. Searching for the truth in the matter. Serving the Light and Will of God to do good for others and proclaim His Holy and Mighty Name. Defeating darkness with every sway of their swords.

Fighting anyone and all things that proclaim they are better than the One True King. For all kings and kingdoms shall all pass away. He and only He shall live forever. In Alastair's mind, his army will fight against the evils of darkness but there would be extensive training. Not only for battle in the physical but there would be training on how to defeat the enemy in the spiritual and the mind. If you didn't know this by now the most clever of the enemy's tricks are the ones he puts in our minds to make us weaker than we truly are. Why would he need to fight us in reality if he could take away the fight altogether? We take ourselves out of the fight by believing his lies. It was Alastair's plan to teach his army how to defend themselves against every evil attack it could think up. Including the attacks on our minds.

Alastair had to keep moving forward. Something kept him pressing toward the truth. He had to find out more about their history. He knew there had to be more to the story that he wasn't hearing in all the tales that he was told. There had to be the truth about it somewhere. Written down for him to read. He had to find out why there were no more dragons in Heaven. His father told him a tale that was passed down through their family about an evil that fell from Heaven with such a force of power that it was seen all across the sky. Like a huge lightning bolt that fell from the Heavens. Ever since then there have been many tales of ancient dragons and their destructive ways. The legends of darkness that have created our present battles. Their stories were always plagued with some materialistic treasure that was out of their reach and some plot derived by darkness to obtain it. The story always ended with a treasure that was just out of their reach and an overwhelming sense of evil's joy in the final moment. However, Alastair always felt like there was more to the story that was being left out. He had to just find it.

Chapter Ten: Truth in the Light

* * *

Alexander, Angelina, and Ziggy still called out to God but He never came to them like He had before. They knew He was there but He never appeared to them. He was unavailable to their eyes. The evidence of His Presence could be seen and felt but the true access just was no longer there. They all grieved their losses in different ways. Alexander sank into his guilt through his deeds and his work. He felt that he had to prove his penance and the only way he knew that he could do that was through his hard work. In his mind, he had to show God how sorry he was for letting the darkness lead him astray from his purpose. That if God was reviewing his case for redemption then God would surely see that he was still worthy of his place in the League of Protectors. Angelina was filled with so much shame and guilt for allowing the darkness to lead her away from the Light that she found herself secluded from the others. She couldn't bring herself joy or peace because she didn't feel like she deserved it. So she refused herself the right to be happy ever again. If God was so upset with her for doing what she did that He would no longer spend time with her then she felt like she wasn't worthy of anyone's attention. She stayed away from the things that used to make her happy. She was no longer worthy of true love.

There is time for everything under the sun. But it never seems to fail that the time after we sin is always the hardest. It's amazing how we can talk ourselves into sinning but nothing we do for redemption can make us feel better for the wrongs that we've done. There is never enough time that can make us feel better about those wrongs. That's where Alexander and Angelina have found themselves. Nothing they could do made them feel better about any of it. Angelina pulled away from Drake. It didn't even phase him. He never even noticed that she wasn't there. Drake was still caught up in his plans for destruction. It honestly made Angelina sad and happy at the same time. Deep inside she had hoped that she was wrong and that Drake really did care for her. But since she decided to pull away from him, it made leaving him a lot easier on her. So they both put their heads down and stuck to only what they knew they were supposed to do. Their jobs and responsibilities in Heaven. But their loneliness made their days longer and their hearts more troubled. Now they had plenty of time to reflect on everything that had happened, which wasn't good for them. It only made the shame and regret louder in their hearts and minds. No matter how hard Alexander worked to make everything perfect, he never felt redeemed for the wrong. However, they didn't know what else to do.

Even Drake could no longer hear from God. But in his own mind, he was so busy plotting his evil out that he never even noticed that God was no longer there. Not having God in their lives speaking to them, it made their jobs very difficult. Because without their direct line to Him, they were not sure what God wanted them to do each day. They were only able to work on what they knew God needed from them from their past experiences. They had to rely on the instructions God had given them before. Without God, their gifts were no longer as powerful as they once were. They felt as if they were just going through the motions of their daily routines and each day that passed made the next day harder to overcome. Even Ziggy's relationship was affected by his sin. He could still hear God but something was different. Nothing had changed. Yet everything felt askew. He could hear God but he could no longer see Him. It was like they were walking in a cold fog in the evening. No light to guide their way. They just had to feel their way through the gray.

What made Ziggy's journey different than theirs? What was so special about him? What had he done differently? Ziggy was just as lost as the other two were. He went over and over it all in his head and there was nothing that popped out at him. From the time that he had entered Heaven until the time when he had gotten upset in the courtyard was no different than Alexander's and Angelina's. The only difference was his sin was greater than theirs and that made no sense! Alexander's fault was that he had questions for God. He had partnered with the darkness when he hung out with them. Getting upset with God? So maybe that was his sin? Angelina could also be guilty of that as well. Associating with the darkness by hanging out with others who were too. Well, she fell in love with Drake, allowed the darkness into her life, and allowed it to control her. Ziggy allowed his frustrations and anger to get the best of him and killed another. But were all of these unforgivable? Would God exile them from Heaven? Would they lose God forever?

Ziggy couldn't let his questions go but he didn't have the strength to ask God anything that didn't pertain to his work. He was worried that bothering God would cause Him to get even more upset than He already must be. That was the last thing that Ziggy wanted right now. If Ziggy had his way about the whole thing it would be like it had never happened. They could all go back to their perfect existence being in God's Good graces and where He was happy with them again. But Ziggy was just trying to make it through each day without making any more mistakes. As they all were. But in his heart and mind, all he could think about was how he felt when he cried out to God and begged God for forgiveness in the courtyard. That moment in time plagued his mind. He couldn't stop thinking about it and he couldn't figure out why. Why couldn't he let it go? It was such a miserable feeling deep in his soul. Knowing he was without God any longer. Knowing he had caused God to be upset with him. Looking back on that day only reminded him of the shame and guilt that had encompassed his life.

The days went by and on the outside everything looked normal. The trees all bloomed their fruits and leaves. The sky was blue and there were no clouds to be seen. The choirs were singing God's Praises and everything was peaceful. They proceeded to pretend like they were happy and doing as God had instructed them to do. But on the inside, everything had changed. The silence in their minds where God would speak to them was deafening.

~ * ~

God knew the moment the darkness came into their hearts. For no darkness could enter Heaven. From the moment He had created the Heavens God's Light filled the space and held back the darkness that has tried to come in. So the darkness found another way into God's Vault. He entered into the only mind that would exalt itself above God. Every other dragon was continuously fortifying their minds and hearts against the darkness. God despises seven things. Haughty eyes, a lying tongue, hands that shed innocent blood, a heart that devises wicked schemes, feet that are quick to rush into evil, a false witness who pours out lies, and someone who stirs up conflict in the community. So in Heaven, we are taught to constantly check our hearts against these things. So the moment the darkness entered into Drake's heart God knew immediately. From that moment on, God kept an ever-watchful eye on His Beloved creation and every step he took.

God watched as Drake allowed his heart to become envious of God and His Power. He saw the moment the ugly vine grew from his heart into Drake's mind where he began to plot and plan. Then as Drake continued to allow the thoughts to remain, they were brought to life through his voice. Which then allowed them to form into action through his hands and feet. God watched as the darkness changed Drake into something he was never created to be. All He could do was watch it unfold before Him like a bad nightmare He couldn't wake up from. One of His beautiful children was being kidnapped in the middle of the night right in front of Him. There was nothing He could do about it. Without Drake calling on God for help, He was left with other options. He could try to talk to Drake and help him through why he was so upset. But when Drake didn't answer Him, He was left with no voice.

Isn't that what the darkness wants to do to us? Leave us thinking God can't help us. That no one can so there is no reason to reach out and ask for help. If Drake would have asked anyone for help with his bad thoughts, someone would have stepped up and helped him overcome the darkness. If Drake had called out to God, He could have talked with him about how he was feeling. God might have been able to diffuse the thoughts before they could've established roots in Drake's thought life. He could have helped Drake take his thoughts captive and purify his mind. There were many things God could've done to help Drake before it got to this moment. If only Drake would have asked.

~ * ~

God could see Alexander's internal anguish. He could tell that Alexander was missing Baldwin. God loved seeing the two of them working and learning from each other while Alexander was on Earth. He knew their friendship was going to last a long time. God could feel the loss in his life. There was no way that one could not be affected by such a loss. When Alexander first entered Heaven he was disoriented and unsure of what had just happened to him. God was happy to have Alexander home with Him but He knew the cost. Alexander gave his life to save Baldwin and Annabeth from the gunfire. He sacrificed everything for them to live. God understood that kind of love. It's the greatest love that could ever be shown. When one knows they are giving their life, to die in the place of the one they love of their own free will. There is no greater sacrifice.

So it would make sense for his heart to be saddened to lose them. But in most cases, the sacrifice was a choice they made in their own free will. So they normally move on easily once they get to Heaven and realize that their loved ones have been saved. However, in Alexander's fury had outside help. The darkness had weaseled its way into Alexander's delicate emotional state and planted a seed of grief and great loss. Once those seeds were planted and started to take root in his mind, all that was needed was a little nudge to keep growing here and there. God figured that the task was up to Drake to quicken Alexander's spirit and encourage it to get out of control. What the darkness cannot stop, it will quicken. It relies on chaos to get things moving in the direction that it wants it to go.

God didn't take Baldwin away. Alexander gave his life for him. God wished that they could stay together but that was not what the cards had laid out for Alexander and Baldwin. But God knew that they would be together again one day in Heaven. One day they would be gloriously reunited and could continue on their adventure. They could catch up and tell each other everything they did and the things that happened while they were apart. They could tell each other about the lessons they learned and the testimonies of the situations that God had helped them through. God knew it would be such a wonderful reunion.

God saw the world differently than everyone else. He saw life as a whole not according to its timeline. He saw a soul according to the fruits it produced in its life cycle. One either produces good fruits or bad fruits. Everything we do and say leaves a print on another's life. We can tell the difference according to how it makes us feel. If we're talking to someone and we leave them feeling encouraged and hopeful, then we are producing good fruits. If we leave them feeling down about themselves and sad about life, then we produce bad fruit. God sees our lives by the fruit we are producing. Good fruits are drawn to the Light. Bad fruits are drawn to death and destruction. Everyone serves one or the other. We can't serve two masters. We are either working for God or the darkness. There can only be one.

God knows the struggle is hard and He is so proud of those who push their way past the temptations of serving evil. Pushing past evil is one of the hardest things you will ever have to do. Because evil is easy. We are born touched by the darkness and it never stops pursuing its claim on us. Once we have chosen to serve the Light, the hunt becomes relentless. So it becomes even harder to get away from it. Especially when it's always whispering in our ears to do its work for it. God sees the battle and cherishes our choice. That's why Alexander's choice to save Baldwin and his family was honored when he died. The love that Alexander had for Baldwin was an act of pure love. There is no greater kind of love.

~ * ~

God could feel the aching that Angelina had for a soul mate. She wanted to feel a connection with someone else. She wanted to feel the kind of love worth dying for. The kind of love that changes everything. She wanted to know what it felt like to wake up and hear the birds singing a newer song. She wanted to fly through the air and know there was someone there to catch her if she fell. God knew that she wanted to feel loved and needed. It was something she never had while she was alive. Her family abandoned her and she gave her whole life to God because of His Love for His People. However, He knew there was a part of life and things that she never got to experience. It was perhaps the only motivation that pushed Angelina closer to Drake and the influence of darkness working in her life.

God loved Angelina like a father loves his daughter. God knew how special she was. He created her to be like no other. She longed for a love that carried the same strength and passion that she was made for. He created her to be mighty and strong. To overcome everything that came up against her. God made Angelina to be faithful, loyal, and unwavering in her convictions. She was to lead and disciple others to walk in the Light and teach others how to tear down the darkness. She was made to glorify God in everything she did. Her joy and laughter was contagious. She was a storyteller and had a wonderful way of entertaining those with her words. She would draw you in and captivate you with her details. He was so proud of her and all that she was created to be.

God knew the love that she was looking for. He knew and had plans for her to meet her true love but the timing wasn't ready. There were some things that God was healing in him that God felt he wasn't ready to be the perfect love for Angelina yet. God's Timing is always perfect. We never want to rush His delicate balance of the work He is doing in someone. You can't rush love. Love takes time. Time to grow into something beautiful and sustainable. You cannot build a foundation on shifting sand. It takes time for a good foundation to turn solid. The same can be said for any relationship. It takes time for love to grow. Some of the best romantic relationships were built by those who started as friends and then grew into something more. As friends, we tend to ask different questions a little more openly than we do with our romantic relationships.

However, Angelina wasn't patient enough to wait for perfect love. God could feel her fragile composure wearing thin. It was getting increasingly harder to keep her settled and waiting. It didn't matter how many times He told her He was working on it, her desires kept the fire burning deep in her soul. God watched as her soul mate struggled with his issues and helped him the best He could. But God can't rush his healing any more than He could steady her patience. Her soul mate was struggling with his own troubles that were keeping them from their happy ending. Again, love cannot be rushed and right now their foundation was being built. They have just become friends and have been through a terrible ordeal. So for now they have to wait just a little bit longer.

~ * ~

God felt Ziggy's heart shatter when his anger got the best of him in the courtyard with Pharamond. God did not make Ziggy to be so hostile towards anyone. Especially to his good friends. But the bigger issue was that God did not create Ziggy to hold all his frustration and anxiety inside till it went nuclear like it did. When God created us, He never would have imagined that by giving us our free will we would have chosen to make such horrible mistakes with it. But then again He is all-knowing and He sees our present, past, and future time. So I guess He did know that Ziggy would do what he did. However, knowing and liking it are two different things. His heart broke too when His Beloved children followed after the darkness and partnered with destruction but from the moment they allowed it to enter their hearts and minds, God had to separate Himself from them. He has to sit by and watch as they work themselves into despair and frustration. He sent others to try and lead them back to the Light but as you can see with Pharamond, it can be very dangerous to ask others to help. Most of the time it is just better to let the course run through and leave it to the Holy Spirit to speak to them and try to change their hearts and minds.

God has been with Ziggy since the day he was born. He had a different life planned out for him. He knew that Ziggy was a little smaller than a normal dragon but that was because God knew that He wanted to eventually promote him to be responsible for the children and kids in Heaven. God created Ziggy's disposition to be happy and to always focus on the positive things in life. Every child would need to be comforted and would need encouragement to look to the future for hope and joy. Of course, they were housed in the area closest to the Throne Room. The area was a big grassy yard with lots of playground equipment to keep them entertained. Because they were not fully developed adults their minds were still young and their new bodies had to represent their child-like thoughts and processing. The singing and the radiating joy from that room were always positive and bright. God felt that was the best place for them to be. Closest to Him.

When He created Ziggy, He created him with the children in mind. He was smaller and more approachable for that very reason. His colors and agile body were created for the children. He knew that they would be climbing all over Ziggy and playing with his features. He created Ziggy to be docile and playful. God knew that Ziggy would be a perfect caregiver for the small ones. Every fiber was designed for this. Including Ziggy's heart. God gave him such a love for little kids. It takes a special gene for someone to love and care for so many children. Even though the children and kids didn't need the physical care anymore they still needed to be entertained. That's what Ziggy came for. He was their constant playmate. He was who they could ask all their questions. He was who they could cuddle with when they needed to be held. He was their dragon.

That's why it grieved God to watch Ziggy make the choices that he made. He knew who He created Ziggy to be and the dragon before

Him now was not the creation He could say He was proud of. Even though Pharamond's death was an accident, the anger and the frustration that led to the event were not. Ziggy allowed himself to get to that point. He may not have meant to get that upset but he did. He may not have meant to hurt Pharamond, but he did. He may not have realized his anger was as deep as it was, but there was no other reason for Pharamond's death. Ziggy allowed his emotions to hurt another dragon. God needed time to figure out what He must do about Ziggy. He had to decide what to do for all four of them.

~ * ~

Ezekiel was lost. He came home to an empty cave. His parents and his brothers were nowhere to be found. From the looks of the cave, they hadn't been there in a long time. The cave floor had more than an inch of dirt and dust on it. The walls were cold to the touch. There hadn't been a fire in the cave for quite some time. The last thing he remembered when he left to go on his bear scout was the cave fire that his mother never let go out. It was always burning hot because she knew her family of dragons would want to come home to a warm spot to coil up and rest. His brother was still sleeping and his father was out hunting for their breakfast before he and his mother woke up. It felt like just another day to him. He nuzzled his mother before he left and flew out the mouth of the cave.

He went on his excursion hunting the bear family, only to come back feeling like a fool. He couldn't wait to tell his father what he had found when he headed home. However, he never made it there till now. Sixteen months after he left. He felt like a different dragon. Because he was. Ezekiel left home in search of food and came home with more questions than he left with. When he left home he felt like he knew everything there was to know about the life he was going to live. But that life was no longer available to him. That day set him on a different path.

When Ezekiel started on his way home he was captured by dragon hunters. Or at least that is what he thought they were. He was captured and his snout was wrapped with a wax-covered rope. He had never seen anything like it before. He had encountered rope before. He had tried to take a farmer's cattle one time from the fence line and they were tied with rope to the fence. He was young and wasn't strong enough to break them from the fence line. That was his first encounter with rope. But the rope that held him this time was warm and the wax kept the rope from sliding and moving on his snout. He tried to break himself free but his small movements made no difference in the rope that held his jaw shut. He pulled with all his might and it would not move or break.

His wing restraints were made of many tight filament wires twisted and coated with wax as well. His tail was held by a large heavy log. His tail was not strong enough to lift the log off the ground. The team that captured him was swift and he was surprised at their efficiency to bind him so quickly. Ezekiel could tell they were trained or at least they were well-practiced in what they needed to do to capture a dragon as big as he. Before he knew it, he was knocked out with some sort of tiny stick they pricked his ear with. A dragon's ears are one of the few spots on a dragon that is not covered with scales. There are a few other more intimate parts that don't need explanation. But they are unfortunately exposed. However, his ears were like large "Come get me!" poles stuck on the top of his head.

When he was knocked out he had weird dreams of a female dragon. She was really old and she was very wise. In the dream, he was floating above himself like he was a fly on the cave wall. He could see what was happening and what they were talking about but he couldn't interact with them. It was as if they could not see him or hear him. He didn't know where this cave was. He had never seen it before this dream. In this cave, he and this wise dragon talked for many hours. She appeared to be guiding him and helping him understand what was going on in his life. He opened his wings at the edge of the cave and he flew out. But she stayed in the cave. He looked back at the opening to the cave and then back to her and she was gone. He looked around the cave to see where she went and she was no longer there. Then the light in the cave started to dim.

The next thing he knew, he was coming out of his dream and he realized he was laying on the cold floor and he was bound in steel chains to the floors and the walls. The walls and the floors were made of wood. He slowly lifted his head off the floor and he felt dizzy. Still wousy from whatever they used to knock him out. He was wobbly and weak in his legs. Every time he tried to stand up he felt like the room was moving and he had to lay back down. It didn't help that he hadn't eaten since that morning and he was starving. He hadn't seen anyone around for hours since he woke up. Just him, chained to this room, and a weak body to keep him company. He lay there and stared at the door. Listened to the weird knocking against the walls of the room. After a while, he realized the room was swaying. Once his mind started to clear and he was able to think better he came to the only conclusion that fits. He was chained in a room in the bottom of a big boat. The swaying was the boat moving on the water. The knocking against the walls was the waves beating the sides of the ship. He didn't know the destination they were headed to and he didn't know why they hadn't killed him yet. Most of the time people captured the dragons for the gold laced in their scales or for the trophies their body parts would bring to their castle walls would bring. He had heard that they sometimes cut off the dragon's horns, feet, and front paws to mount them to wood to put in their houses. Which made no sense to Ezekiel. Who would want a dead smelly animal on its walls stinking up the place? He shook his head and snuffed under his breath.

He found himself bored. He couldn't move very far because of his restraints and even those were starting to wear down his nerves. Needless to say, the view of the wood wall wasn't the most entertaining thing this boat had to offer him. Ezekiel wandered off in his mind. Back to his home where his family was. He knew he was in a bad place but he found peace knowing his brothers and parents were safe in the cave. Warm and happy. They were safe from whoever these people were. He imagined what they were doing right now. His mom was tending to the fire and his dad had just come in with food for them to eat. He was so hungry he wished he was home to get food from his father. Anywhere would be better than this place. He imagined his little brother, Alexander scurrying underneath their feet. Giggling and laughing at Ezekiel. His little brother always wanted his attention. Wanted to play with him and he always had to follow after him wherever Ezekiel went. He knew his little brother looked up to him. He missed his little brother.

He wondered what Alexander would grow up to look and act like. Ezekiel had come to the harsh reality that he may never get to see his family again. He may never know what comes of their lives. He settled into the despair of the unknown. He was saddened by the loss of his family. He wondered if they knew he was even gone from them and in trouble. The last that they knew he was on a hunt after a big bear family and he would be back to the cave later that day. From the best he could tell it had been several days since he had seen their faces. His room did not have a window or access to the outside. So he couldn't tell whether it was day or night. He never had any visitors. No one ever brought him water or food.

Every time he woke from his sleep he realized he had another dream about this female dragon. Every time the dream remained the same but he would learn something new that he hadn't seen before. She never leaves that cave after he sees her. She just fades away to nothing and he can't see her any longer. Almost like she is a mirage in the desert. Or a hallucination from a bad trip after eating the sacred datura flower. Either way, he knew she wasn't a normal dragon. Every other dragon he had ever met or heard about couldn't do weird or crazy things like disappearing. Maybe they could fly faster or they were bigger and stronger but he had never heard of a dragon with abilities like that. That was supernatural. When he was talking with her he felt safe. He couldn't describe it. There was something about her. She was easy to talk to. He was drawn to her. Not for romantic reasons. It wasn't like that. There was something pulling him to find her. The more he thought about his dreams the stronger the feeling got. The only clue that pointed him to know where to begin was the cave. It was the only other thing in the dream that was always constant. The cave never changed.

He felt the boat slowing down. The waves were no longer banging into the sides of the boat. After a while, the boat hit something hard in the front and stopped. He then heard voices hollering out to others to get things roped off and to start unloading the boat supplies to the shore. The next thing he knew, he heard voices just outside the door where he was. The door swiftly came open and someone raised a device and pointed it to his head. Confused Ezekiel sat up quickly and tried to pull against the ropes holding him down in hopes of getting free of their captivity. He never expected it to work, but it did. His wing ropes broke free and he opened his wings. He was tired but with his freedom from the ropes, he was reinvigorated with unexplainable energy. His captors left the large door open and in the hall, he could see sunlight rays pouring in. The doors were very large and swung open to the outside. Which meant if he threw his weight into them, they would bust and he would have the room to open his wings to get away.

So that's what he did. Only when he pushed through the doors did he realize he wasn't in the bottom of the boat. He was on the deck and when he pushed through the doors he was actually out on the deck of the boat in the free air, not in a hall. It looked like something finally was going his way. He opened his wings, pointed his snout to the skies, and opened his wings to the sky. With a big gush of wind, he took off, and into the skies he flew. He flew high into the cloud coverage to get away from the boat and the people. After a while of flying away, he realized he wasn't sure of where he was or where he was flying to. He saw a high mountain and he felt that was the safest place he could land right now. He was also still very weak and hungry. It was daylight and every dragon knew that it wasn't a safe time to be in the air. Once he got to the mountain, he circled it and scouted the best place for him to rest.

He rounded the back of the peak and found a cave opening that was concealed by the ridge and the tall pine trees on the peak line. He landed at the opening and slowly walked inside. The cave air was moist, which was a good sign. That meant there was a pool of water or running water stream through the cave. He slowly walked around the cave looking for the water. He turned the corner of one of the walls of the cave and found a stream of fresh water running down the back wall of the cave. It must be from the melting snow on the top of the mountain flowing through the rock. He was very thankful for this stream. He drank from it for a very long time. Maybe for too long. He was still starving but he was too exhausted to attempt hunting for a meal. It was time for him to rest. Restore his energy. Believe it or not, the boat was not a place he could be at peace and rest. There was a difference between the rest one could get in a safe place and the kind of rest one gets when they are afraid for their life. He closed his eyes listening to the wind swaying the pine tree just outside the cave. He felt safe.

~ * ~

* * *

Angelina found herself alone more than she liked to admit. But she couldn't bring herself to spend her free time with the other dragons. She was too ashamed and still hurt from the realization that Drake wasn't her soul mate. How could she have been so blind? She thought he was the one she had always been waiting for. Wouldn't that have been a grand story to tell? That she had waited all her life for true love and she found her reward in Heaven? Now they both serve the one true living God together forever. She normally daydreamed these stories and adorations of the love that would have been told. Now all they did was remind her of her stupidity. Most of the time she was coiled up in front of her fire trying to forget all of her regrets and it always brought her to remember her time on Earth with the people. She forgot about all the bad stuff by thinking about all the good she did.

Oh, what she would do to be able to go back in time and help people once again. She found herself remembering when she first met God. When she realized that she was phasing in and out of the spirit realm in the cave. Those days were exciting and new. She liked those days. She and God seemed to be best friends. She loved walking with God learning about the universe and that everything had a purpose according to God. It was then that she learned that if all of creation had a purpose to glorify Him then that too must be her reason for living. She then set herself on a mission to guide and lead as many people to God and toward the Light as she could. Angelina spent the rest of her life following the lead of the Spirit and leading people to safety.

She found herself wondering if she could do it again. Not just leading people to the Light but her worry was more about phasing in and out of the spirit realm from Heaven. Would God allow her to use her gifts even though He was upset with her? Would His Grace give her the freedom to use her gifts for redemption's sake? It's been a long time since she has phased. Still coiled up next to her fire, she fell asleep thinking about these things.

When she opened her eyes, she was in the cave again. The more she looked around she wasn't in the same cave. It was a different one. She looked around and she had no clue where she was. She walked around the cave and realized that she wasn't alone. She felt the presence of another dragon. She could hear him snoring. Which was a little disturbing if she was being honest about it. She looked around and close to the back of the cave, she found a small fire needing more wood. Beside the fire was an adult male dragon sleeping. He was a muscular larger dragon. His scales were dark blue with a dark gray skin background. His tail was long and had spikes on the side. A lot like hers. She wondered if he used it in a fight. His horns weren't as long as thought they'd be. His body was large for a young dragon like him. She didn't know how she knew this, but he was really weak and hungry. She put more wood on the fire so he wouldn't get cold and wake up.

When she first opened her eyes in the cave she felt like she was floating in the air. However, now she felt grounded and steady. She left the cave and sat outside the opening for a while to think. She could feel the dirt on the ground. She could feel the wind on her face. She was not a spirit. She was alive on Earth again. She immediately realized this was God's answer to her question. Would God give her grace for her redemption? She felt He was telling her that this was the first step. When she was helping people on Earth before she would allow the Spirit to guide her to help others. Her nudged heart that knew the dragon in the cave was weak and hungry must have been the Spirit guiding her again. She got up from the cliff and went on a hunt to find him food. Once she obtained what she needed she flew back up to the cave.

She flew into the opening, wondering if he was awake yet. He was still coiled in front of the fire. His snore wasn't as loud as it was before. She laid the several deer she'd killed for him by the wall across from him. She knew that he would be starving when he woke up. All of a sudden she felt like she had purpose again. She smiled because it felt good to be close to the Light again. She had missed His Presence and although she knew it wasn't Him directly speaking to her, she felt better knowing He allowed His Spirit to be with her while she was here. It meant everything to know she was back with her true love.

Chapter Eleven: Redemption's Hill

Angelina stayed and waited for Ezekiel to wake up. She was curious about his troubles and how she could help him. But he remained asleep the whole day, leaving Angelina to tend to the fire. It wasn't until the evening that he began to stir. She didn't want to scare him so she partially phased out to give him a chance to become more aware of his surroundings. She didn't know what he had been through and scaring him to death was the last thing she wanted to do. So she patiently waited for the right time to speak.

Ezekiel was waking up from his dream. As he opened his eyes, he realized he wasn't at home, safe next to the fire. But thankfully he wasn't in the boat anymore. For that, he was sure of. He was safe in the cave where he landed to get away from the captors on the boat. He looked at the sun coming inside the cave and from what he could tell, he had slept most of the day away. Which he knew his body and mind needed. However, now it was the needs of his stomach that were screaming out loud at him. But he didn't want to leave the safety of the cave for food. He sat up next to the raging fire. As he was comforted by its heat, he was a little worried because it should have been reduced to a pile of ash by now. So why wasn't it? Alarmed, Ezekiel sat up and looked around the cave to see if he was alone. There was no one in the cave with him.

Angelina could see the worry across Ezekiel's face. She could tell he was suspicious of his surroundings. He kept looking at the fire and then at the cave opening. She could see the thoughts play out on his face. She was worried she had already scared him away. So she decided it was time to say something. She was in front of him, right beside the deer she had gotten him. Ezekiel looked over her way and saw the dinner she had given him. She could tell he was famished by the way he took off toward the meal. She gave him the space he needed to eat in peace. But once he was done eating and beside the fire again, she spoke to him.

"Please don't be afraid. I am not here to hurt you. I am here to help you." She said still invisible to his eyes. She thought it was safer that way. Just in case he decided to attack. He wouldn't know where to attack because he wouldn't be able to see her.

"Are you the one who kept the fire going? And were those your deer I ate?" he responded.

"Yes, I found you asleep and wanted to make sure you stayed warm. If you're anything like me you get hungry after a hard day. So while you slept I got you food." she explained.

"Why can't I see you? Are you a spirit?" Ezekiel wanted to know.

"No, I'm not a spirit or a ghost. I am a dragon and you can't see me because I am partially phased." She felt safe and phased the rest of the way in so that he could see her.

His eyes got big. He must have been surprised to see her there. But it wasn't because she was another dragon or because she had phased in. But because she was the same dragon Ezekiel saw in his dreams. She was the one he had been dreaming about for months while he was on the boat. She was real. She wasn't a dream. Although if he was honest about everything, he was really curious about the phasing in and out. But he kept his excitement contained for now. He wasn't sure as to why she was there but he didn't want to scare her away before he got the chance to ask her more questions and that wasn't the only one that he had for her.

Angelina stood there for a moment so he could get used to her but after a while, she began to have more questions of her own. They began to talk about his troubles. She was there to help him and she needed to know more to know why. He told his story, with every detail since the morning he left his parent's cave till now. He shared the stress of the hunt for the bear family, which was only bait. He told how the captors were skilled and experienced dragon hunters. He unfolded the stress of the boat ride. The hunger and thirst he had to manage. To the escape to the mountain that he now was resting in.

Angelina sat quietly listening to every detail. He only would ask a question if he didn't understand.

Ezekiel only had one last question of hers left to answer. What was his plan to do now? Right now he planned to get back home to his family. To see their loving faces. To take a nap by his mother's fire. To eat with his father and share his story. To coil up next to his little brother and keep him safe from people. Nothing to him was more important than getting home to his loved ones. However, Angelina knew he was not ready to make the trip. He needed more rest and she needed to find out how to help him find his home. So for now he was to stay there till she came back tomorrow. Angelina promised that she would have more for him then. She returned to Heaven and began her search for more information.

~ * ~

When Angelina returned to Heaven she immediately thought of Ziggy and Alexander. If there was anyone that she felt safe to talk to right now it was them. She felt like she had to tell someone about what just happened. She first flew to Ziggy's place. She found him tending to some young ones. They were pretending to climb the mountain. Ziggy was the mountain. They were having quite the adventure. So Angelina waited for him to be free to talk to her. She observed him with the little ones and he really was quite remarkable with them. He was loving, patient, and kind to them. He always focused on their strengths and he never had to raise his voice. To Angelina was a miracle in itself. After a while, she would think anyone would lose their mind with all the kids playing and yelling. Granted they were just playing but still. It would be a bit much for anyone. But not for Ziggy. He was tending to so many of them and she wasn't even counting them. Yet, he was keeping one group calm and listening to him tell stories. Another group he was watching play in the playground area and the last group was napping in the shade near the picnic area. Needless to say, Angelina was impressed.

Before she knew it several assistants came to give Ziggy some relief and allowed him some time with her to talk. In this short time, she had grown a mighty respect for Ziggy that she had never thought to give him before now. She always just thought of him as a happy-go-lucky, free-for-all, playful playmate. Today her eyes were opened and she understood more of God's Heart through His Creation in Ziggy. When God said He made every creature with purpose and with specific gifts He meant every word. Even though Ziggy had made mistakes his gifts were still bringing God Glory.

They sat by the stream and talked about what she had just experienced with Ezekiel. She found herself getting excited as she told Ziggy about helping another dragon in the name of God again. She told him Ezekiel's story of what he had just gone through and Ziggy sat listening with great interest. Angelina thought he was just entertained or maybe he was just happy to have a friend again. She wasn't sure but she knew that it felt good to be talking to a friend again. Her last year has been a rough one. A lonely one. She hadn't realized how secluded she had become being interested in Drake. She couldn't say dating because he never took it any further. So the fault lies with her. She waited so long for him to care and it got her nowhere. It only brought her to a broken heart. A damaged relationship with God. Lately, she has been left with an indescribable loneliness. So this time with Ziggy was healing.

However, that wasn't why Ziggy was so interested. This story sounded so familiar to him. It was like he had heard it before. In her excitement, Ziggy got lost in her storytelling and didn't concentrate on where he had heard this story before. If he was being honest, it felt good to be happy with someone again. He had been sad and upset for so long he had forgotten what it felt like to be happy and to have a friend to talk to. But as she told her story, well Ezekiel's story, he started to realize where he had heard this story from. Its details were familiar because he had just heard some of the same details come from Alexander. He had just Ziggy about his childhood. Growing up without a family because they were kidnapped and Alexander's trip when he got older and had to fly over the ocean for a long time to reach where he thought they were taken. He couldn't contain his excitement and burst into joy as he shared the information with Angelina.

Angelina and Ziggy immediately flew to Alexander to find out if there was actually any meaning to this. As Angelina began to tell Alexander the details of her encounter, tears began to fall from his face. He explained to them that Ezekiel was his older brother. A brother that he had thought was dead a long time ago because he was gone for so long. Alexander was seven when his brother left the same morning his parents were captured. Alexander had to wait almost ten years before he could make the flight to the castle over the seas. In all that time, he had never seen Ezekiel come home. He longed and waited for either of his brothers to come home and take care of him. But no one ever came. He came to the conclusion that they were dead or captured as well. He was left alone to fend for himself. He was lonely, hungry, tired, and afraid most days. It wasn't until he chose to find out what happened and to start training his body to make the trip and to strengthen his body to fight.

He wished he had information about his brother, Ezekiel. He wished he knew what happened to him. Until now he never knew the whole story. He was comforted to know that their paths had crossed and that he was okay. However, it feels like a lifetime ago because now it no longer matters. Alexander was in Heaven, Ezekiel was alive on Earth in trouble, and there was nothing Alexander could do nothing about it. That's when Angelina interrupted him. Because he could help Ezekiel by helping her! That suggestion excited all three of them and they began to get to work. They were on a mission to help Ezekiel. That alone gave them all hope that there was more to their life than all the bad they had done. Their new mission was to help Ezekiel the best that they could.

Angelina explained her abilities to phase in and out of the spirit realm. However, they agreed that it was best not to share with Ezekiel that Alexander was in Heaven. He had to remain focused on what he needed to do. His path was going to be a long and hard uphill climb. They agreed his first step was to restore his strength and energy for the next step. Although they were anxious because he felt like his next step needed to be to go home but, his parents weren't there. They were closer to him than he knew. He was not aware that his parents were captured. He wasn't aware that Alexander had grown up without any guidance. He wasn't aware that Chase's location was still unknown. He wasn't aware that God had a different plan for his life. The darkness may have tried to harm Ezekiel but God had already seen his future and it didn't include his death anytime soon.

Alexander felt like his parents needed Ezekiel's attention but he felt the breeder's army was too large for one dragon. Alexander shared with the other two the details of his death. It was the first time he had been able to talk about Baldwin and Annabeth with anyone aside from God. They needed to know exactly what Ezekiel was facing by sending him there alone. At this moment in time, it wasn't safe for him. He needed help. More help than the kind they could provide him with. They needed an army of resources they just didn't have right now. But they were not without willpower. If they knew anything to be true it was that God would always come at the right time. They just had to start walking their path toward the Light and trust that God was walking before them with provisions.

Angelina had met many different kinds of people on her journey across the world to get them away from wars and to safety. She always told them that if they ever needed her again then all they had to do was to send her a message of a cross and to sign their name. She would know where to go and she would come to their aide. The thought started in her mind, too small to believe it could come to pass. But as time grew and their plans got more involved she knew in her spirit it needed to be done. In her private time, when no one was around, she began sending out her own messages. Near and far they went out in secret.

~ * ~

Ezekiel followed her instructions. He stayed in the cave and restored his energy. It had been a few days and he was beginning to wonder if she was coming back to give him the next steps in their plan. Until today, all he had done was rest, eat, and sleep. He figured the least amount of time in the air would keep him safe from people and other larger dragons. He wasn't sure about what region he was in and he was afraid if he did anything to get him in more trouble might ruin his chances of seeing Angelina again. He wasn't sure why but he was still drawn to her. Like something was pulling him to follow her. Everything in his body was telling him to stay.

In his time to himself, he thought a lot about his family and how he missed them. Although the cave was okay, it wasn't his Mom and Dad's cave. Nothing was like home and even though he knew the journey would be long, he couldn't wait to embark on the road home. He found himself thinking about Chase today. He and his slightly younger brother, Chase, were only a few weeks apart when they hatched. He had always been close to Chase. The morning he went looking for the bear family, Chase had gone out on a hunt for other food for the family right after he left. Since he and Chase were getting older, their father could let them take more of the responsibilities for the hunt. Which his father was kind of happy and a little nervous about.

Ezekiel was worried about how upset his father would be with him for getting captured. His father had taught him everything he needed to know to prevent that from happening. He could only imagine the lecture he was going to get when he got home. He'd hoped by now that they would be happy and relieved that he was alive but you can never tell with parents sometimes. He had been gone a long time. So hopefully that worked in his favor. To be honest, he really didn't care what mood his parents were in. He would be happy to be home and to see their faces again. Which led him to wonder what he should tell them about this adventure. Should he tell them everything? Even the dangerous parts? Should he tell them about Angelina? They probably won't believe him anyway.

He wasn't sure how much longer she was going to be. He was starting to run out of things to keep his mind entertained and thinking about his family and what he should do about things was only torturing him further. Besides that, he could be trying to figure out where he was and how to get home. He knew it was going to be a long trip. He had a lot he would have to worry about and prolonging the planning was not his idea of a good time. The more questions he had the more he found himself wondering about Angelina. Where was she? When she left him where did she go? Was she okay? How could she disappear like that? Could he learn how to do it too? Could she teach him? He had so many questions for her. He was getting anxious for her return. What was taking her so long?

~ * ~

Alexander, Ezekiel, and Chase's parent's names were Conley and Clara. They both were Light Bearers. They knew who they were and their family was everything to them. From the moment they woke in the morning to the time they went to sleep, they knew their responsibility was to care for their precious dragons. Clara always said that her babies were going to change the world. Conley always rolled his eyes at her when she said that. But deep inside he knew they had great futures too. They both did their part to raise them to the best of their abilities. Regardless of the dark madness and pressure around them, they knew the Light was who they were. They were good. They were obedient and they were never caught unprepared. Conley was the neat freak. He always had to have order and organization in his home. Clara was the prepared one. She had a plan for any event that might come up. She was clear and concise in her directions. She made sure that you knew the whole plan in case something happened to her. Conley was the provider. He always made sure her plans were well thought out and that they had everything they needed to make the plan work. They worked well together. They were never caught off guard.

When The Breeder started his plan to capture these dragons, he decided that it would be better to take them separately. He was aware of the family's ability to protect themselves as a whole, but he questioned how well they could do if they were on their own. He observed them as a family unit for over a year before making his plan to take them. His questions worked in his favor. It turned out that they were each harder to capture than he had anticipated. It took more men and all the fortified ropes that he had brought to capture the three of them. He wasn't sure where the fourth dragon went to. He was nowhere to be found and the baby of the family was gone as well. The baby didn't matter to him at this moment in time because it would take the baby years to get to the age he could be used.

When The Breeder realized they were all going to be off on their own expeditions that morning, he set the plan in motion to take each dragon. The first team went after the mother while she was in the cave. It would take some skill and a great deal of strength but if they played their cards right their only trouble would be getting her to the ground and in the cage. They loaded their dart guns and waited for her head to come out of the opening. As soon as she started to exit the cave, the gunman would sedate her with a heavy dose of Valerian root syrup and Kava kava mix. It was a natural sedative that the breeder created in his lab. Dr. Kage Oni was a chemistry teacher in his younger years until the dragon population became too large and he was sequestered by the government to capture and eliminate the threat they had become in his country. The government paid him for many years to kill dragons and when they didn't need him anymore they disposed of him like he was never there. He spent most of his adult life killing dragons, so when he no longer had meaning to the government he sought a different purpose for those skills.

It was then that The Breeder was born. His clothes shared remnants of a college chemistry teacher. Khaki pants, a long-sleeved dress shirt, and a neckline that looked like it used to have a casual tie around it. But now the long sleeves were roughly rolled up to his elbow and the buttons were unbuttoned a few buttons down, and the tie, well, the tie was gone now. He had spent many months in the summer sun where he got used to wearing a brown leather jungle hat that he had worn and made his own. His look was completed with a three-quarter-length heavy leather trench coat and mountain hiking boots for the rough sharp terrain in the Baltic Mountains.

His skills gave him the power to create an army of dragons that would be feared by everyone who had dismissed him as an equal. After he was used by the government no college or business wanted someone responsible for so many dragon's deaths. They felt his shadows were too heavy for them to bear. Rendering him useless to the Eastern way of life. The Breeder renamed himself and set his plans in motion to build a better life. He started off using his contacts to sell a few dragons he had killed to gain some cash and then started buying the equipment that he would need to start breeding and raising dragons for his army. After that, he began hiring men to train to capture the dragons without hurting them. Every day since then, The Breeder paid a finder's fee to anyone who could tell him where people had seen a dragon then he would set forth to capture every dragon for his army.

His chemistry knowledge gave him the power to be dangerous and deadly. Skilled at creating concoctions for tranquilizers was not his only trick. He was capable of making so many things. Explosives, polymers for coating ropes to make them indestructible, and let us not forget the science needed to put specific eggs and dragon sperm together in a female dragon's womb. He planned on making the biggest most feared army of dragons the world had ever seen. So he set out on a mission to find the most unique dragons.

That's when he received a message about Alexander and his family. The details of the message intrigued The Breeder. He left for the region immediately and began his search for their cave. The directions led him right to their front door. The person who made the claim was paid and that's when The Breeder began his research. After a short time, he realized he had struck genetic gold by finding this family of dragons. It didn't take him long to discover that they were very smart and creative. They were a very strong and healthy group. Their offspring would be very constructive to his plans.

The mother was sedated easily and lowered to the carted cage at the foot of the mountain. She didn't put up much of a fight. She didn't have time to. The dart with the sedative on it started working right away. Thankfully it did because the team didn't want her getting too close to the cliff's edge and only to have her fall off to the forest floor below. The father was a little more of a struggle than the other two. The plan to take him was on the forest ground beneath the trees. The Breeder wanted to give the team a safer space to prevent any injury to them or the dragon. Once he was shot with the dart there was always a chance the dragon weighed more than the gunman had calculated. Giving the dragon more strength to take flight into the skies pulling the ropes and the men attached up into the air with him. The gunman's estimations must have been close because the male dragon didn't go under sedation right away and had a little strength to push off the ground for a short distance but because the tree limbs were low to the ground he couldn't make it up too high. Allowing them to pull him down easily.

Once both of the adults were caged the team took off for the last dragon they wanted to capture for the day. They only had brought three of their ships to transport three dragons back to the castle. So after they captured Ezekiel they made their way back to the castle. It would take three months to get there and The Breeder was already planning to return to capture the other two males. It was on the trip back that he regretted not getting the baby dragon. He was captivated by him. His scales had a thin splicing of gold on the edges and a hue of white in his skin. Unique was the only word The Breeder could come up with to describe him. There was something special about him. He could feel it in his bones. His excitement to see who he would become got the best of his thoughts. He wondered if the dragon would display any special gifts or talents. He left wishing he had the time to see this dragon grow up in his environment. But time never worked in The Breeder's favor. Right now his goal was to get these three dragons to the castle.

They reached the castle docks safely but when the team opened the younger male's cabin doors, he broke the ropes and took off to the skies. The Breeder sent a team to find and capture him as soon as it happened. The two older adults were transported there without incident. They were moved from the ships into the castle to their cages as soon as they could be moved. Their cages were deep in the castle basement. The cages are underground, under a castle. The Breeder could be at peace after they were locked down in those rooms. He would only then begin to break their will and teach them to submit to him and him alone. But first, he needed a good meal and a bath. The trip may have been fruitful but his mind and body needed to be left alone. He retreated to his suite and ate in quiet.

~ * ~

Alexander was anxious to know how Ezekiel was doing. It had been several days and he felt like it was time to check in with him. Angelina, Ziggy, and Angelina decided that when their day was through they would meet up at Angelina's cave to go over the final details before she returned to him. The day's workload felt like it was heavier than it normally was. Everything felt like it took forever to get completed and the time dragged on like a snail crawling through the desert on a hot summer day. Angelina was nervous. She didn't want to upset or disappoint Alexander. She knew how important this was to him. She didn't have any family that she knew of but she could only imagine how he must feel about everything. It was hard for her to be in Heaven when she knew he was on Earth in a cave worried and in trouble. She prayed constantly that God would hear her cries and be with Ezekiel and that He would keep him safe in the cave till she returned to him.

For the past several days they spent all their free time planning on what to do next and the details arranged to help Ezekiel move forward with their plan. Alexander was nervous about their plan for him to rescue their parents. Alexander has already met his death fighting The

Breeder in the battle for Baldwin and Annabeth's life. He knew the army and the guns that Ezekiel would one day have to face and it terrified Alexander. He wished he could be there to protect Ezekiel from them. He prayed for his brother and his safety. He prayed that God would watch over him the same way God watched over Alexander when he was in danger. When he was with Baldwin and Annabeth, they taught him about God and how He was watching over him. Baldwin taught him everything he needed to know about God and it still was never enough. Alexander was in Heaven and he was still learning about God and who He is. If it weren't for Baldwin, Alexander wouldn't have ever known who God was and given his life to Him. Alexander began to pray that God would give someone to Ezekiel to teach him about God and no more than he thought that, he felt the Spirit show him Angelina.

That was it! Angelina could tell Ezekiel about God and how Ezekiel needed to give his heart to the Lord. Alexander needed to tell her about this when they met later that evening. Before Ezekiel did anything else, she had to be sure to tell him about God. He had to give his heart to God so that if anything happened Ezekiel would go to Heaven and they would be together again. It was the only thing that made Alexander feel safer about Ezekiel going to battle with The Breeder without him. He didn't want anything bad to happen to Ezekiel but if it did, they had to be sure he would go to Heaven.

Finally, they were able to meet and Angelina and Ziggy arrived at her place at the same time. Alexander flew in right behind them. They could barely get through the opening when they all burst into their thoughts. They all burst out loud, laughing at each other, and fell to the floor. They were under so much tension and stress trying to make sure that they hadn't forgotten a single detail. Their plan couldn't have any holes in it or it would affect everything and Ezekiel could pay for it with his life. So they sat down and wrote down each step as it needed to happen so there could be no mistakes. They all agreed the first step was his salvation. He had to be told about God and had to give his heart to Him. If he couldn't do that then they couldn't go through with the plans. The mission was far too dangerous not to have God on their side.

Tonight would be the night that Angelina went back to him to share the Light with him. Then they would go from there. As Angelina lay down to get ready to leave, they decided it was best that they pray for safe travels and for Angelina to have God's Wisdom and Discernment with her as she told Ezekiel about God. As they prayed, her scales began to glow as the Spirit of God fell upon her and shielded her from the darkness. Alexander and Ziggy continued to pray to God as she disappeared from their sight. Angelina opened her eyes to see Ezekiel coiled at the front of the cave. Almost as if he was waiting for her to fly in.

"Hello, Ezekiel." She softly spoke afraid of startling him. He jumped slightly and turned around to see her standing inside the cave.

"Boy, am I happy to see you! I was beginning to wonder if you were coming back to see me." He exclaimed. She knew he wasn't lying. She apologized for her delay. She had a lot to tell him about what she found out. But as she promised Alexander, her first order of business was to share with Ezekiel the good news about who God is and how he needed to give his heart to God before they could talk about anything else. So Angelina proceeded to fulfill her promise to him and she shared with Ezekiel the goodness of God. He listened carefully to everything she told him about God. She shared with him her story about how she came to know the Lord and how He saved her from all the troubles she could've had to go through on Earth. She explained to him about Heaven and that it was a real place. She told him about her friends and about their jobs in Heaven to reflect the Light to all creatures and how they were honored to serve on the League of the Protectors.

She was surprised because Alexander said that he came from a long line of others who had served on the League but Ezekiel didn't seem to know anything about it. It was like he was hearing it for the first time. She asked him if he had ever heard of the League before and he said that he had. His father used to tell Alexander, his little brother, these tales before bedtime to get him calmed down to rest. These great dragons in our family were all on The League and he was to grow up and be a great Light Bearer as well. But they were just tales from old dragon folklore. They weren't real. She smiled and told them that they weren't bedtime tales. They were real stories of great dragons who served God against the darkness in the world. She fought back the need to tell her about his brother, Alexander. It took everything in her not to tell him that she knew him and that he was safe in Heaven helping her plan these next steps for his safety. But she knew that it was in his best interests for him to not think about his death during the rescue of their mother and father.

Ezekiel struggled for a while coming to terms with this God and that His Son dies to save him from his sins. He was young. He didn't feel like he had done anything that could be called a sin. Alexander worried that he wouldn't make the decision easily. He had time to think it over and he also had Baldwin to guide him and he still had struggles understanding. It wasn't until right before he died that he realized God was real and he heard His Voice in the final moments calling out to him that he believed. So how could they expect Ezekiel to do it at a moment's notice? He told Angelina that if he struggled with this to tell him about his life. So Angelina shared the details of Alexander's life and how he came to know about God. It was hard for her to watch Ezekiel's face after she began because from the moment she said, "Ezekiel, I know your brother Alexander..." his face dropped and the tears started to flow as he learned about his little brother's struggles. She shared with him about the day his parents were taken and how he was left alone for five years. How he began to train his body and mind to make the hardest flight he ever had to make. She shared the details of all his pain and his fears.

She spoke and Ezekiel listened to every word. Deeply saddened by the truths he was now hearing for the first time. He was not aware that his parents were also captured. They must have been on the other two boats beside his in the dock. He did not know that his little brother was all alone and in trouble. More importantly, he was not aware he was gone from his cave for over five years. He knew that he had been held in the ship for a long time but he couldn't believe it was for that long.

Angelina shared Alexander's last few years when he found Baldwin and Annabeth. She told him about his close relationship with them and how Baldwin had shared the good news with Alexander the same way she was sharing it with him today. She told him how Alexander told her that he would struggle with hearing about this God and how he wouldn't know if it were true. She shared with him that Alexander told her to tell him about his life and to urge him to give his heart to God. Even after all of that, he was still hesitant to believe. The whole time she had been talking Ezekiel sat looking out the opening of the cave. He never moved and rarely spoke. He'd ask a question or two but for the most part, he had nothing to say. Angelina went over to him and sat down on the edge with him. She knew this next part was going to be really hard for him to hear and she wanted to be sure he knew she was there for him.

"Ezekiel, your brother struggled with knowing the truth as well. He fought with the idea of there being a God who had the power to prevent all his pain from happening and didn't. He struggled with the idea that if God gave us free will and they chose to hurt others then who would be there for the ones who stood against the darkness? He stood between Baldwin and his family against the evil of other men and finally understood that the Light Bearers were the Protectors of the Light. Alexander died choosing to be the Light for Baldwin and his family. He asked me to give you this as I told you his story." She leaned in and handed him a red ruby that came from the riverbank in Heaven that was shaped like an arrowhead rock. Ezekiel knew then she was telling him the truth. He gave his heart to God and confessed with his lips that he believed just a few moments later.

Chapter Twelve: The Battle

Alastair read the chronicles of The Fallen One's history. He sat still and read each detail of their story as if he were witnessing the events as they were happening. He sat on the edge of his seat captivated by their testimonies. It was becoming clear to him how dragons had become the creatures of the night. There was no convenient time for darkness to enter a life but in their lives, it was well calculated. No life can control how the darkness attacks it but it can keep the evil from spreading. As Alastair kept reading, he began to understand exactly where the deception began in their legacy and it unraveled through their lives with every bad decision they made after.

Alastair needed a break every now and again. It was hard reading about their struggles and the pains that led to their demise. It was easy to judge when he wasn't there. However, it was worthy of the mental and the heart notation in case he ever crosses some of the same experiences. He was, after all, wanting to learn from their mistakes. Alastair was hoping to figure out some sort of plot made by the enemy. Maybe a common connection or a habit that would give the darkness away. He knew there was a reason for him to be drawn to these books; to this library. He felt like the key to everything was here. He just had to see to it. Search it out. Like any good Berean, He would find the truth of it all. It was all in God's Time. He took his break and sat in the garden at the bottom of the tower. The garden relaxed him. The stream that flowed by the library was rocky and its rough flow cascading down the hill was calming to his mind. It never changed in all the years he had been coming to read these old books. The sounds always put him at ease when the world raged on in his life. He could always count on the library to soothe him. He wondered often if The Fallen Ones had a place like his that calmed him and gave them rest. Maybe if they had their stories would have been different.

Alastair could read their testimonies and see the epic battle for each of their souls being played out right before his eyes. The darkness would make a move, while The Light would maintain control the whole time. They always fought so hard for each of the dragon's attention. However, after this last attempt for control, it appeared that nothing the darkness did could steer them back to it. At least that's the way it was looking. Would the darkness give up and leave them alone to seek redemption? Or would it make more attempts for their lives later? Alastair wasn't sure how their stories would play out, but one thing he did know. The Light always wins. Anxious to know the ending, Alastair returned to the tower and continued to read their stories.

~ * ~

If there is one thing you have to know about the darkness that lurks in the shadows is that it is always watching and waiting for you to make a mistake. That was where Drake found himself. Lurking in the dark places trying to figure out what the three dragons were working on. He wasn't happy that they weren't hovering over his every move anymore and let's just say he was waiting for a way that he could stir up trouble. So as the three continued with their mission to help Ezekiel, they noticed they had an unwelcome guest around every corner. So their actions had to reflect even more discretion than they already had. They had to protect the mission at all costs.

The one advantage that they had over Ezekiel is that Alexander had already been to the castle and even though he hadn't walked through the inside and did not know where his parents were, they were confident God would make a way. Ezekiel was left with very simple instructions, stay hidden and be safe for now. Nothing would ruin the plan more than if Ezekiel got captured by The Breeder. However, it wasn't easy. Ezekiel was getting a little stir-crazy alone in the cave. Even hunting at night was getting lonely and it used to be one of his favorite things to do. When he was younger he used to fly through the trees at night and pretend he was being chased by a monster. He would fly through the air and he'd use his most evasive maneuvers to outrun the beast. He would feel so alive and invigorated as he rounded every corner and once he chased down his meal he would point his snout to the skies and swoosh through the clouds.

Those were the days when he could live young and be free. Not a care in the world. Those days were long gone and everything was different. Now he had to worry if the monsters were real and if they were chasing him in the night sky. He knew The Breeder had to be upset that he got away from them at the dock and he could only assume that he sent out a team to find him. So staying alert was vital to his existence. He wished he had more information about all of the plans the team had but Angelina said for now it was better that he only know the parts that he needed to be responsible for. It would be less confusing and she wouldn't have to worry about him trying to do things out of order.

In the meantime, Angelina, Alexander, and Ziggy continued with their parts of the plan in Heaven. There was a lot of information that had to be gathered and not that much time to do it. Angelina had to phase into the tower library to find out the exact size and rooms in the castle. Once they attacked the gates they wouldn't have time to search every room. They would have to limit their search to only parts of the castle that were big enough to hold animals of that size. She was also responsible for finding out all she could about the surrounding area. According to Ezekiel when he flew away from the boats that transported him there, he was flying maybe thirty miles north of the castle. If they could find a map of that region, they might be able to plan their attack a little better. Angelina was doing everything she could to run down all the information they needed to give to Ezekiel. While maintaining her duties in Heaven. Now was the time for her to make sure she had spent time in her secret place, glorifying God. He may not be talking to her right now, but if He was listening she wanted to be sure that she was prioritizing her love. She never wanted to be in that place again where she put others or other things in front of God. So in her quiet time, she spent her time lying at His feet and singing His Praises. For no one was worthy of all her love but Him. She knew that to be her truth and her heart would reflect that for the rest of her days.

Including her listening to the still small voice telling her it was important to secretly call on those she had helped on Earth. She wasn't sure if anyone would come but she knew in her heart that it was what God was calling her to do. She wasn't going to let Him down and not listen to His instructions. So her secret messages went out in private all over the world. She was calling on all who would come to their aid. There were so many different types of people with different stories and pasts. She could never find the time to ever tell someone about them all but she knew they had faithfulness to the Lord. She sent out the messages resting on the fact God would call who was needed to their side.

~ * ~

The Breeder was still unsuccessful in finding the dragon who had escaped his capture at the docks. He knew their family was smart but he wasn't really aware as to how fast they were. He stood on the docks as Ezekiel soared into the clouds away from them. Thankfully Ezekiel was far enough in the clouds that they couldn't see in which direction he had gone. This dragon piqued The Breeder's interest because his flight skills would be a wonderful gene to pull for his final creation. He had never seen a dragon as fast as he. He hadn't had the time to take a close look at Ezekiel because he rode on the main ship with larger captain's quarters but as Ezekiel climbed in the air into the clouds, it looked like there was a flint of gold laced in his scales just like his younger brother's scales were. This made Ezekiel more interesting as time went on because the dragons with gold had special skills. He never knew why they were different but all across the world the dragons with this detail were special. He wanted to get a hold of one to look at their DNA under a microscope. He knew this meant something. All meaning to one's life was found under the microscope and in science. There was a reason for everything and he was going to find the meaning for this out.

In the meantime, The Breeder had other dragons to tend to while his men were out searching for him. Currently with the two parents, He owned and controlled 6 dragons. If he could get these two under his control and get the one that just got free caught, he would have nine. He had plans to send his teams and vessels back for the other two dragons once they were restocked. The Breeder felt good after this last catch. The female dragon has already had hatchlings before. So she won't be as vicious as the younger females he controlled. Once her spirit is broken, she will continue her purpose in life, which is to give birth to more dragons for his army.

~ * ~

This testimony infuriated Alastair as he read it. Who was this man to think he could tell a female spiritual being like a mother dragon that she was anything aside from who God had created her to be? She was a magnificent creature to be held in the highest regard. Oh, he was mad. This man was buying and caging dragons only for the money and power they could make him. He was trafficking these beautiful creatures like cattle in the stockyards. Did he not know that God created them to be protectors of the Light? That their purpose was not to give him hatchlings? He was angrier than he had ever been. He had to take another break, only this time he knew that he needed to go and spend some time with the Presence of God. It was in God's Presence that he would find the answers he needed for the anger and hate that was building in his heart over this man. He knew it was a testimony from the past but still. It upset Alastair. Maybe more than it should have. But he had to God to find out why and how to deal with these feelings. The accounts of what this man was doing to these dragons were unbearable. It broke his heart. He had to go to the Father with this in his secret place.

It was in God's Presence that Alastair learned who he should be mad at. Yes, the things this man was doing upset God too, but it was the darkness that caused this man's change. So nothing but the Light could stop his evil ways. He had to be stopped and his empire had to be torn down but God was dealing with him in his time. This past testimony of The Breeder's life was only a fraction of the evil the world has dealt with. Today Alastair was facing the same evils with different faces and names. But it still needed to be stopped and in his secret place, God showed Alastair what he needed to do to fight against the evil he faced. But not before he finished his reading. God told him he had to go back to the library and finish the chronicle.

* * *

~ * ~

Angelina had completed her research and gathered her information for Ezekiel. The three dragons set down a time to go over the next steps together and to pray again. Alexander was supposed to gather information about where Baldwin's house was and how close was it to the castle. Alexander did not want Baldwin and his family anywhere near this battle. Putting them in danger was the last thing he wanted to do. However, this battle was going to be too big for the region and Alexander had to point Angelina to them so that she could send word to Baldwin to get out of there before it began. Ziggy was still helping Angelina with drawing out the maps. So during this visit with Ezekiel, all that was going to happen was she was to tell Ezekiel his next steps and then she needed to go to Baldwin's house to warn them. Everything seemed pretty simple. Or at least it should have been.

It took Alexander no time at all to point out on a map where Baldwin and Annabeth's family home was. The rest of his time he began obsessing over the worry he had for Ezekiel and The Breeder who was seeking him. He was beside himself, stressing over what could happen if his older brother got captured. The more he thought about it the more it the sicker he began to feel. His nerves were shot. He couldn't sleep. He couldn't eat. All he could do was freak out. Nothing calmed him down. He had no one he could talk to. He wanted to talk to God but He hadn't answered in a long time. He still didn't know what he had done to make God so mad at him, but God still wasn't answering. So there was no point in trying to talk to Him. He gave up trying anymore a long time ago. He couldn't figure it out. So he just gave up and moved on. But the worry over Ezekiel was affecting everything in Alexander's day. It was all he could think about.

Angelina, Alexander, and Ziggy gathered at Alexander's cave for the meeting. Alexander said he wanted it to be there so that he could have a comfortable place to sit while she was gone. They went over the details of all that she needed to do and they began to pray. Everyone closed their eyes but Alexander. Everyone started to pray out loud but Alexander. Angelina felt the Spirit enter the cave and she felt the warmth cover her. She began to glow. She began to phase to

Ezekiel and then about halfway through the phase she felt a jolt of energy push her down and she fell into the cave. She rolled over and there was Ezekiel. His eyes were as big as rocks and his mouth was wide open. She stood up and closed his mouth.

"What is wrong Ezekiel?" she asked as she dusted herself off. Ezekiel just stood there and pointed behind her. She turned around in the cave to realize that there was another dragon in the cave with them. At first, she thought this dragon was with Ezekiel already in the cave but given his demeanor and the surprised look on his face, she came to a quick realization that this dragon had come through with her. Defensively she asked the dragon to get up and tell them who he was. The dragon stood up and stepped into the light streaming into the cave.

It was Alexander! Oh, my goodness, it was Alexander! Angelina began to freak out! She began screaming at Alexander. What was he doing?!? What was he thinking?!? After all of her frustrations came out she plopped on the cave floor in the corner and began to shake her head in unbelief. There stood Alexander fully grown across from his older brother, Ezekiel. Ezekiel did not know this dragon. Although something about him seemed familiar to him. He cocked his head to the right and looked at him like he was trying to figure it out. This dragon was tall like his father and he kind of looked like him too. But his coloring was different. This dragon had gold thinned in his scales just like he did. He turned and looked at his scales then back to this other dragon's.

"Ezekiel, it has been a long time since we have seen each other," Alexander said to Ezekiel hoping he would finally recognize him. "Do you know who I am to you?"

"No." He replied looking to Angelina for a hint or a clue. However, she sat there still shaking her head. He looked back to the dragon and was looking for an answer.

"I am your little brother, Alexander."

Ezekiel plopped down on the floor and his eyes got big again and he finally understood why Angelina was so upset with him.

"I have been hearing about your troubles from my friend, Angelina. I have been sick with worry over you. I could no longer sit by and not help you. Believe me, you're going to need a lot more help." Alexander sat down next to his brother.

"Mom and Dad have been captured by The Breeder. I was captured by him too, but I got away. This guy is bad news. His weapons are like those I have never seen. His ropes are light and yet stronger than heavy metal. They are unbreakable. The people are smart. Smarter than they usually are. They're stronger than they usually are. I don't know what to do. I can't do this alone." He hung his head and cried with his brother.

Angelina wasn't sure what to do now. She had always thought that being able to phase again was only because God was giving her favor to redeem herself. So what does this mean? God is not ever tricked nor does He allow something to happen without His permission. So in that logic, God must have allowed Alexander to phase through to help his brother. Not that she wasn't happy that he was there. She was. She only hoped that he was there to help him and not put them in more danger. She could only have faith in the Father that this was the right move to make at such a crucial junction in their journey. However, since he was here he could make the journey himself to talk with Baldwin and Annabeth. Angelina would continue to other parts of the plan that needed her attention while she was there.

The other two didn't know this but she really needed to see the castle from the inside. She was worried because no matter where she looked she couldn't find any blueprints or plans about the castle. It was built long ago and there were no official records kept over the years. Once they were inside they would be without any guidance and that wasn't okay with her. She didn't want any surprises that day. So she limited the unexpected by planning for everything to go wrong. But she didn't want to take the chance with other's lives in her hands. She had to use her phasing gift to find out where his parents were being held and the only way that she could do that was to phase around the castle to see for herself. Once she phased through the main gates, she could walk freely as the halls and doors would allow. Invisible to the untrained eye. All they would see would be whatever was behind her. She felt that this was the needed edge to making this day successful.

Once she had gone over their plans with Ezekiel and Alexander, she set off on her way to the castle. She did not share with them her plan to go there. She just told them she had some other much-needed business to tend to and would see them in two days. Ezekiel's cave was not far from the castle so she made her way in the night. Flying in the dark sky drew less attention and she could remain undiscovered for most of the journey. She found herself wondering about the depth of her abilities. For most of her life, she had spent most of her time on foot. Rarely in the skies. Her job was to help get people to safety. It's hard to do that when they're unable to fly also. As her wings spread open as she took to the skies, she was encouraged to try something that she wondered about over the years. She could phase out of visibility while on the ground but could she do it while in the sky as well? Once she was close enough to the castle to see them she felt it was a good enough time as any.

She went a little higher in the clouds and gave it a try. As she was climbing into the clouds she saw a lighthouse with glass mirrors in the baffles to reflect the light out through the seas to serve as a warning to oncoming ships would know there was land in that direction. Without another dragon to tell her if it worked she had no other way to tell while in the air. Her best bet since it was night was to fly close and then once she could see she would immediately fly up into the clouds for coverage. Just in case she was spotted by people on the ground. She phased out and headed back around towards the lighthouse. As she was flying back, something caught her attention. There were other dragons in the air up closer to the top of the mountain. As she looked around she noticed the castle facing the ocean cliffs. She thought she had better phase out now before trouble erupted. She phased just as she came onto the lighthouse and as she passed by the mirrors she saw nothing reflected back to her and that brought a smile to her face.

This new skill gave her a great advantage as she planned her next steps. As she landed nearby, she noticed that the castle had a lower gateway entry at the back of the bottom of the castle. Possibly for entrance for the captured dragons or other large deliveries to come into the castle. Regardless, it was a perfect entry point for her to get in and cause the least amount tif disturbance. Besides she needed the space and room that people did not require to enter. She decided to wait nearby in the trees till later in the night when the people had hopefully calmed down and gone to bed. The less traffic there was in the hallways, the better it was for her to explore. So as time slipped into the night she found herself under a very large pine tree with heavily weighed branches that gave her coverage from eyes that might walk by. She needed some sleep before she went inside the castle. As the night came softly in around her, she nodded off for just a few moments.

She hadn't been in a deep sleep for very long before she opened her eyes and there sat Ziggy staring over her. "Hello." He said with a smile on his face.

"Hello?" she answered giving her time to wake up and get up off the floor.

"That wasn't very long," he said as he got up and went to the fire to add more wood to it for her. "I thought you would be gone longer and I wasn't aware that Alexander was going along too."

"Well, I wasn't aware of that part of his plan either. I was just as surprised as you were. But I figure that God wouldn't allow it to happen if He wasn't aware. He would have to approve something like that, right?" Angelina asked still shaking her head in disbelief that Alexander had done that.

"Your guess is as good as mine." He said rolling his eyes about it all. "I am glad you heard me calling you because I wasn't sure what to say or do about Drake. He has been by here asking where you were. I told him I thought you went on a walk around the perimeter making sure everything was okay. But he looked very suspiciously at me as he left. I figured that I better call you back here to check in with him. You know? So he'll stop snooping around? What do you think?" Ziggy said as he looked out the cave opening to see if he could see Drake.

"Yeah, that makes sense. Good thinking. Do you want to walk with me in case he starts asking more questions? You can say you went and found me for him."

As they started walking through the courtyard, Drake flew down in front of them. "Hello, you two. What are you up to?" Ziggy responded that he went and found Angelina for him since he was wondering where she was at. Drake rounded in behind them, almost like he was inspecting them for the truth.

"Yeah, I went on a walk around the perimeter to check on things and make sure everything was okay. It had been a long time since I had made a perimeter walk and felt like it was my time to do it. Don't you think?" Angelina chimed in looking at Drake over her shoulder.

Drake comes in around on the other side of Ziggy and asks them if they want to go and do something together. When they didn't respond quickly he answered the question for himself. "Oh, that's okay. I understand you both have a lot to do these days. Don't stress over little ole' me. I'll find something to get into." He spreads his wings and takes off up into the clouds headed toward his cave. Relieved they both flew back to Alexander's cave. Angelina knew she had to get back to the castle but she didn't want to leave Ziggy defenseless. She was torn but at the same time, she had a habit of underestimating her friends and their abilities. She knew Ziggy was responsible and he definitely was capable. She just wasn't sure she could handle losing another close friend. But she had to trust God with his life. There was nothing she could do if all their plans and hard work fell to pieces because she couldn't be disciplined enough to stay on task.

"Ziggy, do you think you'll be okay till we return?" Angelina caringly asked.

"Yes, I believe we bought ourselves some time with Drake. I will maintain the story till you return. If something goes astray, I will call you home like I did earlier. Okay?" Ziggy responded.

"Okay perfect. I was in the middle of a big research project and need to get back before I run out of time." Angelina said as she wrapped her wings around Ziggy and squeezed him. "You're a great friend to me, Ziggy. I am thankful to God for bringing you into my life."

She thought about the pine tree next to the castle and phased back to her spot underneath the tree branches. She wasn't sure of the people around and the light situation anymore so she phased invisible. Just to be safe. Thankfully it was still deep into the night and she wasn't noticed as she returned to the tree. Unfortunately, she lost the spare time she needed for rest. So she maintained her invisibility to enter the castle. As she entered through the lower-level gates, she noticed a dank murky odor filling the halls. She couldn't quite place the smell. It wasn't familiar to her. It didn't smell natural to her. She was aware that The Breeder used to be a chemistry teacher, so she was sure that whatever she was smelling wasn't something God had created but man-made. Bad man-made, if you will. She noted the smell and continued through the halls.

As each door was opened, she was able to look into each room down the hallway. Carefully staying out of sight and assessing the rooms for the captured dragons. Most of the rooms were for people who worked there in the castle with The Breeder. A majority of them were strong men. Nothing really to report or note. Aside from bad housekeeping and smells she wished she could get out of her nose hairs but still no dragons had been seen. She wandered down each of the branched hallways searching for them. The deeper she ventured into the castle the darker the rooms became. No windows in the rooms any monger for the rooms were encased by the dirt that forged the cliffs. She did notice that the darker the rooms became their furniture that was in the room was no longer nice and well built but instead roughly made and dirtier, maybe a better description would be dustier. Almost as if the rooms hadn't been lived in for many years.

You can learn a lot about a person by the rooms they live and sleep in. You can tell the station or class of person that you'll be dealing with by the way they keep their belongings and by what they own. A stable hand doesn't make much money so they don't have the extra money to spend on frivolous things that they don't need. Most of the time they have several changes of the same clothes, several pairs of boots and hats. Their room more than likely will have a special nice saddle in the corner on a stand that they saved their hard-earned money for. You'll see several bottles of alcohol and glasses to serve friends who might visit. But overall their lives are spent in the stables tending to the animals they were responsible for. A chef who is responsible for the food served in the castle is often paid better than a stable hand. So they can spend their money on some nicer things in their room. Nicer clothes, shoes, and apparel. They might have more nice casual clothes to wear outside the castle to shop for produce and items they will need in the kitchen. So when they go to town they reflect their employer. So the employer pays them more to represent him.

In this case, most rooms looked like the stable hands rooms. Rough and dirty. Clothes flung in the corner of the room. Papers and bills were thrown on the rough tables by the bed. Ropes coiled and hung on the hooks on the walls. Muddy boots piled behind the door, out of the walkway. However, there was a suite that was at the end of the hallway on the upper floor. This person owned the castle. IT screamed The Breeder lives here. Books were everywhere. Books about different animals and the genes that made them who they are. Microscopes with many different slides in a case beside the scope for easy viewing. Papers pinned to the walls of a cork board with formulas and equations written all across it. There were large glass containers holding cut off dragon parts; teeth, heads, and feet. There were horns and claws hanging on the edge of the chalkboard. There were cold boxes of glass that were holding blood and fluids keeping them cold. This room had a huge balcony and a view overlooking the ocean from the cliff. The balcony was large and had a table and chairs outside for eating. The balcony doors were big and heavy. You could tell it would take a mighty force to break through them if they were closed, but they were both standing wide open to allow the air to move through the room. The curtains were made of a thick velvet material that would block the sun from the room if you wished. Everything in the room had its perfect spot for it to belong. Nothing looked disorganized or out of place.

She spent a long time in this room. Maybe too long for before she knew it, the main hallway door to the room opened and a tall dark-haired man walked in. Surprised by his entry, Angelina hid behind the chalkboard with some of the papers taped to it. She was still invisible but she worried it would still not be enough. So she hid behind the board. As she stood behind the board, she could smell cigar smoke from his pipe. He sat in his red armchair and stared out the balcony at the ocean. She stared at him for a while watching to see what he would do or say while she was in there, but as she stared his way she realized she was staring at pictures on the back of the board. She backed away from the board to get a better view of what she was looking at and she almost gasped as she focused on the content. She was looking at pictures of all the dragons that The Breeder had in captivity. She gazed at a dozen dragons and read the details of their lives or their capture. Each dragon was unique and skilled in some way. There were many equations and science formulas that she could not understand but there were some written details of The Breeder's speculations of the genetic markers in each of these dragons. There were several pictures that caught her full attention. There was a picture of Ezekiel and an older male dragon that she assumed was his father. There was a picture of a female dragon and a very young dragon that looked a lot like Alexander. Then there was a single picture of a black dragon who looked a lot like Alexander and his family. However, his eyes were darker and his face was meaner. She didn't know who he was but she knew she hoped he wasn't in the cages too. He wasn't a dragon she wanted to mess with. She looked a little longer and saw blueprints of an underground cave that he had made into a housing unit for dragons. Cages were built into the mountain to keep his dragon army. They weren't being kept in the castle. They were being kept there and that is where she must go.

She followed the dark hallway of the lower part of the castle to where the dragon caves were located. A few minutes in she realized the dank, dark smell she was smelling in the house was getting stronger the deeper she ventured into the caves. The smell was stronger and the air got colder. Dragons will only burrow deep in the ground in the caves when they are looking to hibernate or to protect their young ones after they are hatched. Not many creatures will come that deep into the cold Earth. The colder the ground gets the more dragons want to curl up to get warm and go to sleep. The cold calms them. Makes them sleepy. The cold wet air is a natural sleep agent to a dragon. What a wonderful way to exploit a dragon's natural weaknesses. Control an animal by controlling its environment.

Thankfully for Angelina, there weren't a lot of people working during the night. She didn't have to worry so much about being seen or being bumped into while she was in the halls. However, if there weren't many people needed in the caves apparently there was also no need to keep a lantern lit. So the halls were darker and spookier than she cared to admit. Obviously, the castle staff wasn't instructed to dust and clean these halls as much as the house because the cobwebs and dust were not helping her feel better about what she was feeling. She just kept telling herself that if she got in trouble, all she had to do was phase back to Heaven and she would be safe again. Even then her skin hairs were still standing on their ends. She found herself repeating, "Lord, please protect me and keep me safe," under her breath. But nothing could prepare her for what she was going to see next.

When she got to the end of the long hallway the end opened up. It had a big heavy metal door that could be shut and reinforced but at this time it was standing wide open. Propped open with a big wooden wedge against the cave wall. The cave opened into a huge open-air room underground, almost like a terrarium. The cave stalagmites and stalactites were dripping with natural water. The air smelled salty like the ocean but stronger. The mountain stone walls must be the only thing keeping the ocean out of the caves. There were heavy metal cages lining the room walls. It appeared the trained dragons were able to walk, fly, and roam free when they didn't have other orders to do something else. However, there were some dragons that were locked in their cages. Granted they were big cages. Big enough for the dragon to get up and move around to a different position but not enough room to stand up straight or spread their wings open. They didn't look too comfortable. They looked very tired and hungry. Malnourished to say the least. I guess that was one way to break their willpower. Starve them till they submit completely.

There was a small hole in the top of the large cave room. Not man made but a large break, almost circle-like. The cave walls went straight up through the mountain. She believed the back side of this mountain used to be an old volcano that was no longer active. Although dormant the stench of sulfur and burning rock still filled the air. That was the smell she couldn't place. It had to be. Along with dead dragons, blood, and other unmentionables all together in one place. The den of horrid evil was too much for her to bear any longer. She found out what she needed and she had to get out of there before she made a scene. She spread her wings and up through the top of the volcano, she exited swiftly. Her mind is still unable to process all that she saw but she knew she had to get back to Ezekiel and Alexander quickly to tell them all about it. Her wings couldn't get her to safety fast enough.

~ * ~

Alexander and Ezekiel were able to make it to Baldwin and Annabeth's home just in time. It took them a lot longer than they expected. Flying to their home when you're trying to remember how to get there in the first place was quite a challenge. But they made it. Alexander was so excited to see his brother he hadn't planned for the emotions that would flood in as he saw them for the first time since his death. So when they landed in front of the house and Baldwin burst through the front door because he couldn't believe his ears, they both were overwhelmed with tears and joy. Baldwin and Annabeth ran to him and wrapped their arms around him and they flooded Alexander with a lot of questions. Then the fear set in, because he remembered why he was there.

At the same time, Angelina landed next to them all. White as a ghost and a little shaken still by what she had just seen. They all were alarmed by her face and her inability to speak. "It was worse than we had expected. The Breeder is pure evil. I don't know where he is getting his motivation but he needs to be stopped." She cried out.

"Angelina, slow down! What are you talking about? What happened?!" Alexander put his wings around her and tried to calm her down. "Tell us exactly what happened." He said as he asked her to take a deep breath.

"When we were in Heaven I did all I knew to do to try and find out information about The Breeder's Castle. I looked everywhere. I couldn't find anything. So I took it upon myself to phase into the castle and look around." She explained to them.

"Why would you do that? They would spot you in a heartbeat and shoot you on-site." Alexander questioned her.

"Ever since I was younger, helping people get away from danger I have always wondered if I could be invisible while I was flying. So I gave it a try, and I can! So last night I made myself invisible and flew to the castle and got in. Maintaining my invisibility I was able to walk around the castle unnoticed. But you will not believe what I found!" she explained to them about the chain of events that lead her to fear. She told them about the captured and tortured dragons in the cages. She told them about all the pictures and the science The Breeder had in his room on the board and on display. Then she told them about the horrible smells and the dead dragon bones everywhere. She told them how horrible it was and how she had to get out of there because she was going to be sick. She was terrified to go back.

"Did you see my parents there?" Ezekiel asked.

"I couldn't get down to where the dragons were caged to see if I recognized nay of them. But I do know this. He has pictures of your whole family on the board and he wants to capture you all. His board had a lot of science formulas on it that I couldn't understand but I think he thinks your family is special andhe want to know why. There were pictures of you two with your parents and there was a picture of another male dragon that looks like you all but he was darker and mean looking. Apparently, he is related to you and was the first of your family that he had captured with gifts. It didn't say what any of your gifts were but that you all had them. Alexander, I think he knows about our gifts from God. You know our special talents."

"Don't all dragons have soecial gifts? Baldwin asked them.

"No, Baldwin. Not all dragons are strong, fast, or can disappear like Angelina and I. There are only a specific group of dragons that have these special abilities. They are called The Chosen. They were given special gifts when they are young to learn so when they mastered these gifts and became obedient to the Lord, they would be chosen to serve on the League of Protectors with God in Heaven one day." Alexander explained to them.

"He must want us for our gifts to breed an army of evil dragons. But how does he think the gifts are given? It's endowed by God in the birthing process. Only God knows and can endow those specialties to those He deems worthy. You can't create them in a lab..." Alexander said speaking to himself as he questioned The Breeder's endgame.

"Because if I can build an army of my very own specialty dragons then I would be the most powerful man on Earth. My dragons would be feared by all. I could use them for whatever I want. I could take down governments. Bring nations to their knees all in my name." The Breeder said as he landed his mightiest dragon in Baldwin's field. Right behind him, five other dragons landed to his aid. All seeking blood. All looking to kill. All looking to destroy their enemies in front of them.

Angelina noticed the darker meaner dragon from the board was the one that The Breeder was now riding. Alexander and Ezekiel recognized him too. He was riding their brother, Chase. Chase didn't look like himself. Something was wrong. Did he know that they were his family? Alexander reached out his wing to go and talk to Chase, but Angelina and Ezekiel held him back. He turned and looked at Ezekiel as if to say we have to help him. Ezekiel just shook his head quietly in disagreement. Clearly, Chase wasn't being made to help that madman. Chase crouched down to allow him to get down then stood back up and straightened his disposition of authority. The Breeder climbed down off his saddle and stood before them, smoking his cigar.

Angelina backed away from the front of them closer to the back. She was aware of the danger that was about to erupt into this very small field in the hollar of the mountain. She knew their strengths and their weaknesses and right now the biggest worry was if these dragons attacked with their fire, Baldwin and Annabeth were at a terrible disadvantage. The closer she could get to them the better she felt that when the battle began she could shield them from the fire and phase them out of harm's way just like she phased with Alexander. She looked around hoping to see the boys that Alexander had talked about. Their young, wild imaginations and play in their past made for some amazing tales. But they were nowhere to be found. Maybe they were somewhere safer than there. At least she hoped.

Alexander looked at the dragons facing them. It was six against three. Six dragons trained to kill and destroy others. Dragons who were rewarded for the evil they could cause. They were a small army made for only one purpose. To dominate others who stood in The Breeder's way and right now it was Alexander and his friends. As he stood there listening to The Breeder talk about his obsessions and plans, Alexander began to notice there were people stepping out from behind the trees in the mountains, the house, and the barn with weapons. Alexander was worried. That was more people than he cared to kill for his loved one's lives. He had been here before and it didn't end so well for him the last time. There were more than him that time too. The field was overtaken by evil and it's will.

Angelina felt the despair come across her heart. They now were overcome by an army of thousands. She looked at Baldwin and nudged him to come closer. He walked her way and held Annabeth's hand as he walked. The tension was building by the second and they all felt the darkness growing as he explained his plan to torture and dominate those who came against him. Every word that came out of his mouth carried the intent to bring fear and despair to them. The dragon's wing tips were planted in the ground in front of their bodies preparing to launch when called. They growled as they waited. Chase just stood there, smiling like he was finally going to be better than they were. His jealousy and pride were an ugly attribute Ezekiel had all too quickly forgotten. Alexander was too young to remember the torment that he caused. But Ezekiel hadn't. He had always hoped he would change but there was never any sign given that said that was ever going to happen. They stood quietly and listened to the wind howling in the trees. It sounded like a low hum of an army. Oh, oh, oh oh. Oh, oh oh oh. Oh oh oh oh…The night had been long and they were all tired. Alexander, Ezekiel, and Angelina were ready to stand their ground. They were going to stand against this evil. They may not have been the most perfect Light Bearers but they knew where they had gone wrong. They knew who their God was and they were there ready to die in His Name. God was God and this man was not. The hum got louder. Accompanied by the faint clash of a sword grip and a shield tapping in rhythm.

Angelina was prepared to move quickly. Alexander stood at the point, ready to take on anyone who came at them first. He was by far the biggest and the strongest of their group. Ezekiel was off Alexander's right side, ready to protect and fight. Angelina was off to Alexander's left. She was the closest to the house and she was ready to disappear to the cave with Baldwin and Annabeth then return quickly to the fight. Alexander felt his heart rate speed up and he saw time slow down. He rose in the sky above his body and he could tell he was having another vision of the future. He hadn't ever been able to repeat this since that day that he and his friends had the race in the forest and he saw himself winning. He saw The Breeder and his dragons running for their life in great fear. He saw Chase and The Breeder flying away up into the clouds. The Breeder screaming that this wasn't over and that there would be hell to pay for this. Alexander smiled and he entered back into his body in the present and he started to run towards the enemy.

The Breeder drew his sword to commence the attack and lead the dragons and all the people who came to help them attack the dragons and lead them to victory. He raised the sword and began to yell, "At ––ta––ck!" when Angelina began to phase. Everything from here out happened in slow motion. Not sure why. Maybe because she was phasing with people? Or maybe God wanted her to see what she saw next. But as they began to phase out of visibility, they saw something their minds could not explain.

The Breeder and his small army of dragons were not all that stood there growling and gnashing their teeth. With them and beside them were an army of evil spirits and demons taking charge as well. Angelina, Baldwin, and Annabeth were seeing directly into the spirit realm. The demonic forces of red glowing eyes and claws tearing at their own flesh and tearing their tattered clothes. Their voices screaming and screeching ungodly sounds. They could see only six dragons but with them they carried such an evil presence that was unfathomable. Within a quick second from behind the demonic forces they all of a sudden see the sunrise through the trees in the mountain. Angelina looked to Baldwin on her right and she could see the people coming out from behind the trees stepping into the sunlight. All of a sudden they began to reflect a Light from the sky that Angelina had only felt in the warmth of Heaven when she radiated God's Pure Light. All these people were Light Bearers and they were repelling the evil and the darkness away from them!

At that moment she instantly knew they were on the right side of this battle! She stopped the phase and brought them back to the battlefield. She began to scream with all her might, "Light Bearers, Move Forward!" In that glorious moment, the three dragons, the people who came and answered her message for help, and the angels whom God sent to their aide ran toward the evil ones and brought forth a battle cry that has never been heard before.

Part One

Chapter Thirteen: Judgment Seat

Chapter Thirteen: Judgment Seat

While the Light was pushing back the darkness on the mountaintop, Angelina phased back into the castle while it was left unguarded and set the captured dragons free. Among those in the cages were Alexander and Ezekiel's mother and father, Clara and Conley. The rest of the dragons were released from captivity and set free to return to their homes. Angelina got to meet them and see their family partially reunited. They got to return home with Ezekiel and got to say goodbye to Alexander. They were proud of him but saddened by his departure at the same time. No one ever wants to lose a child but they understood he had to return with Angelina to Heaven. They were thankful that God let them come home just one time to help Ezekiel and Baldwin against The Breeder. Although, he was gone from the picture they were sure that would not be the last time they would see him.

Angelina and Alexander had gotten close during this adventure. She cared for him deeply. She wasn't sure what that meant but she knew she didn't want it to change. He was a great friend to her now. She didn't want that to end. She didn't want to go back to normal. She didn't want to go back to the quiet, loneliness that awaited her in Heaven. She didn't want to return to not having a purpose and a meaning in her life. She wanted to see her friends and Ziggy again. She had missed him. He had become a trusted friend and someone she could talk to. She missed God more but He wasn't talking to her anymore and until she figured out how to make it right, life in Heaven was hard. It was like she was always trying to guess if she was doing what God wanted her to do. Without direct access to Him, all she could do was guess. She didn't like guessing on the things that were so important to her. It made her feel sick to her stomach.

She liked it better when she was alive on Earth. At least then she had the Spirit to speak to her and to guide her. On Earth, she had friends to talk to and help. She wished that her time in Heaven wasn't so tainted with unhappy memories. Drake made sure of that. In Heaven, he was everywhere reminding her that he didn't love her and that he didn't want her. He never said that out loud but the rejection was still there. In her mind, it was there and she just wanted to get away from it. Away from Drake. But she knew that wasn't possible. It was time for her and Alexander to return to Heaven and their responsibilities there.

She hated having to pull Alexander away from all those he loved. He finally felt like he had his family back and they had a lot of time taken from them. Alexander had a lifetime of grief that he was never going to be able to get back to him. A lifetime of getting to know his parents and his little brother better. Everything he knew of them until today was what he knew when he was seven years old and the mind of a seven-year-old doesn't see or hear things the way an adult does. They don't ask the same questions and they don't observe the same things. He wanted to know who they were now. He wanted to know how their experiences had affected them. Who did they turn out to be? Were they happy with who he was? Did they regret not being there for his life? There was so much they wanted to talk about. Things

Alexander wanted to know about them. But there just wasn't any time left. Who knows, there may never be enough time because the past is gone. It was done and there wasn't anything they could do to change the present. All they could do was keep moving forward in the life that was given to them. Keep pushing towards the goodness and the Light. Unfortunately, it wouldn't be together. Alexander would go back to Heaven and his family would stay here on Earth to finish their testimony. They promised that they would always go towards the Light that way, one day they might be together again in Paradise. Until then their paths came to a fork at the foot of the mountain. His path led into the hills to the Light and their path continued in the Valley through the forest.

Angelina and Alexander went to the cave where Ezekiel was hiding out in. They figured it would be as good a place as any to depart. They didn't want to make it a long goodbye and they definitely didn't want to make it a big ordeal. It was going to be hard enough on them as it was to leave, knowing they wouldn't see them again for a very long time. So they just wanted to quietly disappear from Earth and quietly enter back into Heaven. Little did they know, their absence wasn't unnoticed. Everyone was talking about it. Everyone but God. There is nothing that He does not see. He knows all and sees all that goes on in the universe. He knew when they decided to push Him away and walk in darkness. He knew when they were upset with Him and had all these questions they wanted Him to answer to. He knew when they realized they had made a big mistake in allowing the darkness into their hearts and their minds. He knew immediately when they wanted to do good again. God knows every move we could ever think of making and where our hearts are positioned when we make them.

God knew when Ziggy repented and asked God to forgive him for his mistakes. It is through his repentance that God knows that they are ready to move toward the Light again. Without that repentance and submission to His Will can God truly know when they've learned their lesson? Without remorse for their sins, they would continue down the same bad path to destruction and death. It is only through God and the Light that we can have true peace and life. Free will had consequences for the actions they had taken. They weren't aware of what was to happen next but they knew they needed to get back to

Heaven to answer for them.

Angelina was thinking that she was still on a good path leading to redemption. That her good works would put her back in God's good graces. Alexander wasn't so sure. He knew he had done wrong, deep in his heart for leaving Heaven. But he just felt that he had to do something to help Ezekiel and his parents during this difficult time. He hoped that God knew his heart and that he was sorry for his disobedience. Ziggy felt sorrow for his mistakes every day of his life. He took the life of a dear close friend who was just trying to help him. Pharamond's face was burned into his soul forever. There was no amount of goodness that he could do to be redeemed for this. He knew in his heart he was not worthy of forgiveness. However, it did not stop Ziggy from asking God for his mercy and grace every day for the pain he had caused. With Drake, well he still did not care what God thought. He felt nothing in his heart for his sins because he justified them as righteous. He felt he had done nothing wrong. He felt he did what was necessary to achieve his goal. He still felt that he was better than God and it was that pride and arrogance that had led to the sins of others. That was his mistake. Thinking he was a God and had the power to hold others accountable to him. When in reality we are held accountable to the judgment of only one true living God and His Opinion is all that matters.

The battle on Baldwin's field was a great victory. Evil's destruction was stopped for a short time and The Light was seen by all who charged the enemy. Alexander got to see Baldwin and Annabeth one more time before saying goodbye and returning to Heaven. So when it was time for them to go home, Angelina and Alexander began to phase away from Earth to go home to Alexander's cave. But when they opened their eyes they were not in the cave. They were in the entranceway to God's Throne Room. Standing beside them were Drake and Ziggy. They all seemed to be surprised and their worry was written all over their faces. They stood there in complete silence waiting to go in. They all knew in their hearts the wrongs that were committed but they had somehow managed to give themselves a false sense of security. Settled in peace in the knowledge that God loved them and that His Mercy and Grace were abundant to His Children. But they had never seen the side of God that simply would not allow a wrong to go unchecked. He had given them plenty of time to step away from the darkness and stop making their acts worse. However, none of them stopped. They did not heed His Warnings.

If you look all through history, God has always sent a prophet or a messenger with a warning to a person or a city that was about to receive His Judgment. In the case of Nineveh, he sent Jonah with the warning. It was well received and His people turned and repented right away, immediately stopped their wickedness, and begged God for His Mercy. They were saved and allowed to live. In the case of Sodom and Gomorrah, he informs Abraham of His Judgment that is coming. Long story made short, there were no righteous that could be found in the whole city and angels were sent to bring forth their judgment of sulfur and fire. God always wants us to stop giving in to our desires of the flesh and live for a higher calling to please Him.

An archangel came out of the Throne Room gates and motioned them to come in with his arm stretched out and his palms up. As they entered the Throne Room, God was seated in the middle on His Throne. Jesus was seated on His right hand. All the archangels were seated at tables on a lower level in front of them. Their tables were facing each other. One of the tables was on the left side and one of the tables was on the right side. On the tables, there were many books laid out and opened up in front of them. The choirs that were normally singing God's Praises were there, but their heads were held in reverence and they were only humming His Praises in this moment.

As the angel was walking before them, he slowed and turned with his hand palms up motioning them to stand at the altar before the tables. Drake walked in first. Prideful and arrogant he walked in with his head held high, like he had nothing to be ashamed of. He looked at the archangels like they were beneath him. Them being there was ridiculous and uncalled for. He stopped at the altar railing and snarfed as he stuck his snout in the air. The other three dragons were not so confident. They knew what they had done wrong. They were wrong in the way they were thinking and in the things they had done. They were ashamed of themselves. They all stood at the table. Not really prepared for whatever was going to come next.

As the archangels began to speak, they started reading from their books the detailed accounts of all four of their lives and all that he had done. One by one they read each of the dragon's accounts. They started with the good and then they read from the books about the bad. With each of the four dragons that were in front of the court, the archangels read from all the books. Each dragon had their life slowly unfold before them as an angel read out loud the sum of their events. Nothing they had done or said felt worthy of the weight they were now feeling in their soul. Everything came down to this one moment in time. Every word that was ever spoken and every motive of their hearts was laid on the scales before the Lord. Each dragon hung their head low as they felt the weight upon their shoulders with every detail read for the court to hear. In all their training, nothing could have prepared them for this day.

Drake stood with his head still held high. He had known God the longest and he felt like he knew how this was going to go. God would give them some slap on the wrist punishment for their disobedience and they would go back to work making Heaven the perfect place for people. God was a loving and caring God. He was their creator. His punishment wouldn't be that bad, for He was a good God. He was known for His mercy and grace. Drake felt like he was safe. This was just some formality to get them to step back into order and become afraid of God once more so that they would listen to Him. He listened as all the accounts were read and then his mind began to tune out the reading and he began to plot out what he was going to say that was going to get the court's attention to overthrow God from His Throne. You could almost tell that he was no longer listening because his thoughts of what he thought he was going to say became clear to everyone when he began smiling and looking mischievous. His pride was getting the best of him. You would think that since he knew God the longest, that he would be afraid of the wrath that God could carry. History has always shown us that God's judgment was not something to be taken lightly. But that did not carry any weight in Drake's mind and heart.

Angelina stood there and all she could do was quietly cry. She knew they were in trouble and she also knew that God was upset with them. She was terrified, not only for herself but for her close friends who stood there with her. She didn't know if there was enough grace and mercy for the pain they caused and the severity of their disobedience. Tears just fell from her eyes and down her cheeks as she awaited their judgment. Her head hung down in shame as they read her life's story. She wished she could escape and not hear anymore.

Alexander stood there as calmly as he could. Not ashamed of all his decisions because the decisions he made in the end saved his loved one's lives and whatever God deemed fit for his punishment he would just have to live with. He truly felt in his heart that he needed to come back to Earth and help Ezekiel. If that was the last thing he ever did for his older brother, then so be it. In his heart, he was sorry for allowing Drake to confuse him and get him angry with God. Now as he thought about it, he felt the repentance come over him. He was sorry for the times he got upset with God. He allowed the darkness to enter his heart through Drake's suggestions. He should have questioned what he was hearing before accepting the lies as his truth. Because even though he did not like the fact that he had died, he knew in his heart that it was his choice. It was his sacrifice for them to live. That alone meant everything to him. He chose to die so that they might live. God was not to blame for that. That was not God's fault. He wished he could change everything that had happened. God was correct when he told Alexander that there was pain down both paths. No matter what he chose to do on Earth would have led him here to this judgment seat. He just wished he had been a better listener to God once he had gotten to Heaven. If he had just stayed away from Drake none of the other bad stuff would've happened.

Ziggy, however, was lying prostrate on the floor. For he knew all his wrongs and he felt them deeply every day. There was no describing the horror he felt deep inside his soul for the judgment he knew was going to get. He didn't feel like he deserved God's grace and mercy. But he had no clue what he could do to ever redeem himself to God. For he wasn't worthy of His Love. His mind and heart have been toiling over the matter since it happened and nothing was ever enough to Ziggy. He had humbly repented for his sins. He had asked God to forgive him. If he could talk to Pharamond once more, he would beg him for his forgiveness. Ziggy had hurt him so badly and he wished for nothing more than for that life to be resurrected and be made whole again.

~ * ~

All three of them had realized all their wrongs as they sat there and heard the accounts that were brought before the Lord. Each of them was in a different phase of their journey. There were not two that were alike. Each life had a different set of experiences that led them to the judgment seat. Their paths had variables that affected them in different ways but they all carried one remaining issue that needed to be dealt with. They all had to forgive Drake for his part in their story. They all were left with an anger that they had for Drake leading them down this dark path that they never were intended to be on. They knew that they were to stay away from him because he had caused all this mess and they were sure to check their minds and hearts for any darkness that could creep in again. But they were forgetting the unforgiveness in their hearts that they were holding onto for Drake.

Unforgiveness was such a hidden ugly seed that evil would use to rob them of any joy in the future. Not only could it continue to steal their joy but it could cause their spirit to hinder in its growth. Because of that bitterness of unforgiveness, these four dragons would never walk in the righteousness that they could if they forgave him. So then they would never be truly free of the darkness. For their hearts would be stained carrying that. Any friendships made from here on out would be affected by this decision.

After their lives were read out loud the court began to speak to God about the matters that were important for God to hear more about. There were times in their lives when the books didn't give exact details as to why those actions or words were taken. The angels wanted God to hear more about the story because they felt these details were what God needed to know to make an informed decision. Although, it was clear on His Face that He knew all and was aware of all things that were before Him. But He heard what they had to say anyway. When they were done speaking, He heard from His Son, Jesus. Jesus was for them. He made His case before God. He explained that He had died to save them from their sins. He reminded the Father that they had repented for their sins and that His life was given for theirs.

At that moment, the books on the tables in front of Alexander, Angelina, and Ziggy began to flip through their pages. The crystal clear waters from the River of Life came from up out of the stream into the Throne Room and washed the pages clean of their ink. The ink washed out of the books in blood-red ink and flowed back into the stream bed with the rest of the water. The pages were once stained and now they were as white as snow. Jesus smiled for His Love for them was great. His death was His sacrifice for their souls. However, now they had to go before God. They stood before God and in His Silence He said everything that He needed to say with His Eyes. As tears fell, He closed His eyes because He knew what He needed to do. The four immortal dragons that stood before Him disappeared from the Heavens. They disappeared from the court and fell into the darkness on Earth for eternity. Stripped of all their armor, helmet, and shields. As they fell from Heaven like a lightning bolt, they were stripped of all of God's magnificence and glory. Their skin and their scales darkened. Drake was stripped of all his powers and strength. He was weakened and his fire no longer burned as hot as it once did. Angelina, Alexander, and Ziggy were stripped of their armor and strength but they were allowed to keep their gifts but they were left with a warning.

The warning God left them with was this. You will continue to redeem yourselves. You can keep your gifts to continue to do good. To share the Light. The moment you give into the darkness again, you will be stripped of all your gifts forever. As they fell from Heaven, God separated them to different parts of the world away from each other. Ziggy was sent to the Orient. There he lived out his life leading others to the Light. Helping people become the Light Bearers they were created to be. He helped warriors bring honor, peace, and wisdom to their families during times of great struggle and turmoil. Alexander was sent to the Northern Baltic countries. Reunited with his parents and Ezekiel. They decided to live in the cave near Baldwin and his family to aid their paths in the Light. They served the Light for the remaining years of their lives. The two boys grew up around many other dragons. They both served with dragons and both became great riders. He serves them with great honor and respect. Teaching others how to be the Light to others and how to maintain peace in the region. Angelina was sent to Greece where she continued to lead people to God and help them be the Light for all to see. She uses her powers only to travel to see Alexander and Ziggy, but she is no longer allowed to go back into Heaven. For God stripped them all of their access to Heaven. They can no longer hear directly from God. They only have access to His Spirit here on Earth. So through the Spirit, they can speak to Him. However, she lives near the ocean and flies over it as much as she can. Helping ships and boats see the coastline.

When they were cast out of Heaven and back down to Earth, each of the three dragons agreed to live out their years serving the Light. Doing good and helping people get to know the one true Living God and His Ways. However, there was one left who did not want to return to the Light and because of his stubborn, prideful ways, he continued to roam the Earth causing wars, famine, and destruction wherever he went. Some have said he killed Chase and became a slave to The Breeder. Others have said he fell into a pit of great darkness and went to sleep away from people and the Light. Never to be seen again. However, all dragons have been told of Drake's fall. Because after he was cast out of Heaven he was no longer worthy to be mentioned ever again. But all Light Bearers know the truth of his future. For a prophet has spoken of it in the last book.

~ * ~

Since the beginning of time, there has been a raging war for our souls. The darkness has done everything in its power to keep us from serving the Light. To keep us from being a Light Bearer. To keep us from sharing the Light with others. It has sent sickness and disease to weaken our bodies. It has destroyed our property and our belongings. It has sent demons to mess with our minds and change our thoughts. It has made us feel inferior, unworthy, unable, incapable, unlovable, unforgivable, unqualified, misunderstood, defeated, and alone. Those are the biggest lies that we hear from the enemy. For God tells us that we do not fight against flesh and bone but against powers of darkness and principalities that rule the Earth. If we're living in God's truth over our lives and according to His Word then we are none of those things and neither are those who are coming against us. So we cannot wage war on them, take your power and your authority against the darkness, and send those demons back to hell where they belong.

Angelina, Alexander, Ziggy, and Drake had sinned. Drake's greatest sins were not his pride and his arrogance. Drake would not repent and change his ways. He grew into the dark and he refused the Light. Everything he did was to tear down the Light from other's lives. Alastair felt the weight of their judgment in his soul as he read their testimonies today. He cried as he read their truths and felt their pain of the destruction the darkness had caused them. As Alastair finished the books, he sat back and reflected on what he had learned from their lives. He reflected these truths as he wrote them in his heart as an experience he could never forget.

Always listen carefully to the words other people speak to you and over you. Weigh them on the scales of your heart and compare them with the Word of God. If they do not encourage you and build you up in your relationship with God then it is best to dispose of it quickly. Always follow the Light. In times that are confusing and chaotic, remember to seek after the Light on your path. It will never fail you or lead you in the wrong direction. God is your first love. If you are seeking to find a mate make sure that God is their first priority. If God isn't their first priority then they aren't going to love you in the way you need to be loved. How could they? Seek after God in all your companionship needs.

Evil is always crouching in every shadow seeking to kill, steal, and destroy your ability to share the Light. What he can't stop he will accelerate. Wear your helmet at all times. Make sure you watch for foxes trying to steal your good fruits. For the darkness can enter your mind and plant seeds of deceit. Manipulate your mind to perceive things in the wrong way, and make you feel things that God doesn't intend for you to feel. Truth is always brought forth in the Light. Redemption's Hill is always a hard journey. If you find yourself needing redemption make sure that it's for God's Glory not for you. If you seek God's advice first, He can save you a lot of time and energy if you would just go to Him before every decision.

Last but not least, God created you. He created you to be a Light Bearer and He is always calling you to His Side. No matter where you are on your journey, He wants you to be safe from harm and He wants you to have a blessed future. He loves you and wants you to join Him. He wants you to be who HE CREATED YOU TO BE. We all have a choice on whom we will serve. The Light or the darkness. Now it's up to you. Who do you serve?